Reunited at St. Barnabas's Hospital

Love is blooming in the leafy heart of London

The sun gently rises over a tranquil Richmond Park, but inside St. Barnabas's world-renowned neurosurgery unit, sparks will soon be flying. From the tension of the operating rooms to the emotion of the rehabilitation center, Barney's talented surgeons and doctors give their patients their all— and find love when they least expect it!

In *Twins for the Neurosurgeon*
by Lousia Heaton

When neurosurgeon Samantha Gordon went to work in Paris, she never expected to fall for fellow neurosurgeon Yanis Baptiste—or fall pregnant with twins! Now they're working together in London. Could the family of their dreams be within reach?

In *The Doctor's Reunion to Remember*
by Annie Claydon

Dr. Clemmie Francis recognizes Dr. Gil Alexander instantly—seven years ago, he rocked her world, then disappeared without warning. Gil's amnesia means he may not remember what happened, but the attraction between them is impossible to forget!

Both titles available now!

D0974859

Dear Reader,

Memory is always subjective—two people can remember the same set of events very differently. One of the many challenges of memory loss is that while others can help fill in the gaps, everyone's assessment of a particular event is different. When Gil and Clemmie meet again after seven years apart, Gil struggles to come to terms with a shared past he cannot remember, and Clemmie has to reassess what her own memories really mean. Now that she understands why Gil hurt her so badly, should she tell him about all that she's been through or keep that knowledge from him?

This book was close to my heart, and being able to give Gil and Clemmie the happy ending they deserved gave me particular pleasure. Thank you for reading their story, and I hope that you enjoy it!

Annie x

THE DOCTOR'S
REUNION
TO REMEMBER

ANNIE CLAYDON

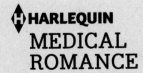

MEDICAL
ROMANCE

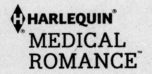

HARLEQUIN®
MEDICAL
ROMANCE™

Recycling programs
for this product may
not exist in your area.

ISBN-13: 978-1-335-40884-6

The Doctor's Reunion to Remember

Harlequin Enterprises ULC
22 Adelaide St. West, 40th Floor
Toronto, Ontario M5H 4E3, Canada
www.Harlequin.com

Printed in U.S.A.

Cursed with a poor sense of direction and a propensity to read, **Annie Claydon** spent much of her childhood lost in books. A degree in English literature followed by a career in computing didn't lead directly to her perfect job—writing romance for Harlequin—but she has no regrets in taking the scenic route. She lives in London: a city where getting lost can be a joy.

Books by Annie Claydon

Harlequin Medical Romance

Dolphin Cove Vets

Healing the Vet's Heart

London Heroes

Falling for Her Italian Billionaire
Second Chance with the Single Mom

Resisting Her English Doc
Best Friend to Royal Bride
Winning the Surgeon's Heart
A Rival to Steal Her Heart
The Best Man and the Bridesmaid
Greek Island Fling to Forever
Falling for the Brooding Doc

Visit the Author Profile page
at Harlequin.com for more titles.

CHAPTER ONE

IT WAS A brisk uphill walk from Richmond Station, and Dr Clemmie Francis was a little out of breath by the time she got to St Barnabas's Hospital. The large modern building sparkled in the sunshine, and Clemmie turned left at the main entrance as she'd been instructed, walking towards the older building that stood next door.

The neurological rehab unit was an example of a previous reincarnation of Barney's. Grand in quite a different way, with high arched windows and fancy brickwork, that would have been a state-of-the-art example of a modern hospital in Queen Victoria's reign.

Clemmie was a little early, so she crossed the road and sat down on a bench that was placed on the border of Richmond Park. She imagined that the windows of the neurological rehab unit afforded a magnificent view of the park, and that it would be possible to see for miles from the top floor of the building. A smile found its way from her heart to her lips. Seeing for miles was exactly what she wanted to do.

For too long now, she'd taken each day as it came, facing each new challenge as it presented itself. It had been a matter of self-preservation, a way to ignore a future that seemed to hold only jarring reverberations from the past. But slowly she'd made a new start. Found a place to live, scraped old paper from the walls and made it home. Found a new job, at a neurological rehab unit attached to a central London hospital. She'd been determined to shine, and she had.

And now she was on a fast track to promotion. The head of the unit was due to retire in six months, and Clemmie would be his successor. Spending six weeks here at Barney's, which was recognised as one of the best neurological rehab units in the country, was an opportunity to learn and prepare herself for her new role.

Clemmie filled her lungs with air. The future really did seem to be waiting for her, sparkling in the early morning sun. She took a moment to appreciate the feeling of anticipation, and then got to her feet. Turning up early on your first day was never a bad thing, and she just couldn't wait any longer.

The entrance of the older building gleamed

in quite a different way from the main hospital complex. No vast sheets of glass or shimmering automatic doors. Here the pace seemed a little slower and quieter, and it was the polished wood of the lobby that caught the light. Beyond that, a large, bright space, where Clemmie could see a woman sitting behind a reception counter.

'Dr Clemmie Francis. I'm here for the director of the unit…' Clemmie handed over the letter from her hospital's administrator, who had dealt with her placement here at Barney's, and which instructed her to be here at nine this morning.

'Ah! Yes, we're expecting you.' The receptionist grinned. 'You wouldn't *believe* how many people have turned up here this morning instead of where they're supposed to be. You're in the right place though. I'll give Dr Alexander a call. Sit down right there.'

Dr Alexander? A name from the past, which even now had the power to send shivers of agitation down Clemmie's spine. She turned, obediently walking over to the seat that the receptionist had indicated and sitting down.

It was nothing. How many Dr Alexanders were there in this world? More than one, clearly, and this one would probably be middle-aged and avuncular, if the welcoming style of the reception area was anything to go by. Or a woman, maybe...

Clemmie took a deep breath, going through all the reasons that this *couldn't* be the Dr Gil Alexander that she knew... Scrap that, the one she'd met seven years ago, had a brief fling with and clearly hadn't known at all. He'd be somewhere in the fast lane, getting his kicks from emergency medicine. That, or sitting back in a comfortable leather seat with private patients hanging on his every word. Maybe back in Australia...

Enough. Wherever Gil Alexander was, he was part of her past now. She'd moved on and she didn't need to wonder about him every time something happened to remind her of *that* mistake. The first domino to fall in a succession of others that had brought her world crashing down.

'You'll be with us for a while...?' The receptionist's voice came to her rescue and diverted her attention.

'Yes, six weeks. I work at the Princess Victoria Hospital in north London.'

'Ah. Nice.' The receptionist shot her a blank look. 'You'll like it at Barney's. Everyone's very friendly. And if there's anything you need, just come and ask me. I'm Maggie.'

'Thanks…' There was one thing. 'Could you tell me where the ladies' is, please?'

'Back there, turn left, and the lockers and the ladies' room are right in front of you.' Maggie jerked her thumb, pointing behind her. 'If you want to pop there now, Gil said he'd be five minutes.'

Dr Alexander. Gil. *Dr Gil Alexander.* Shock must have impaired Clemmie's reasoning ability, because she was already on her feet and halfway over to the door that the receptionist had indicated before she put it all together. And even then she was groping for some reason not to believe it. Maybe *this* Dr Alexander was Dr Gillian Alexander… No, Maggie had said *he*.

By the time she got to the washbasin in the ladies' room, her hands were shaking, and she turned on the cold tap, dangling her fingers in the stream of water.

A warm summer, much like this year's. Sticky heat. Sweat. Gil doing things with her body that she couldn't forget, however hard she tried. She'd met him at a two-week conference and liked him…a lot. Fallen into bed with him with embarrassing speed, and then believed him when he'd said that he couldn't wait to see her again. That business with the photo booth, where they'd had their pictures taken and written their telephone numbers on the back, had been just cruel. He'd never called her, and when Clemmie had called him, excited to hear the sound of his voice, he hadn't picked up. She'd been embarrassed and belittled, as well as hurt.

She stared at her reflection in the mirror above the basin. What if he recognised her?

What if he didn't? That could cut both ways: it would be a blow to her pride, but it would make things easier. She could pretend that it had never happened. If he started to make her nervous, she could employ the old interview trick of imagining him naked...

Which wasn't going to work. Imagining someone naked was supposed to empower you. The Gil she'd known was far more powerful naked than he was clothed.

Imagine him as a liar. Someone who breaks his promises.

That wasn't going to be so difficult—Gil *was* a liar. Clemmie splashed a little cold water onto her cheeks, drying her hands carefully. She had to think clearly. Gil had made her feel so miserable, so humiliated, that her work had suffered. She'd pulled herself together and resolved that would never happen again. Now more than ever it was important, because this six-week placement meant so much to her.

If she was just one in a long line of forgotten lovers, then it was simple. Clemmie would

pretend it had never happened. If he did recognise her, she'd play dumb and pretend she
didn't remember him.

She picked up her bag and opened the door
of the ladies' room. The reception desk was
still hidden from view, but the sound of a man's
voice made Clemmie stop in her tracks.

She was sure now. Even after all these years,
Gil's voice sent shivers down her spine. An
Australian accent, softened by years living in
London. The sound of a smile in his tone.

'That philodendron's looking a bit sad, Maggie. Aren't you going to water it?'

Maggie chuckled. 'I thought *you* were the
gardener around here. And I can't leave the
desk...'

Clemmie heard him laugh. She'd liked that
laugh so much...

She should probably breeze back into Reception as if nothing were amiss, but that just
wasn't possible. If seeing Gil had as much effect on her as hearing his voice, then she needed
a moment to breathe. She tiptoed forward and
caught sight of him.

Gil was standing with his back to her, examining the large plant that stood by the entrance
doors. Still broad-shouldered and slim-hipped.
His hair was a little different from the neat
crew cut he'd had when Clemmie had known

him, and had grown out into a mass of dark curls. Just that brief glimpse of him left her breathless with shock.

'I'll go and get some water. I've got some plant food in my office—that'll give it a pick-me-up.'

'I'm sure it could have waited until lunch-time, Gil.' Maggie reached under the reception desk, producing a glass jug and putting it on the counter. 'And stop insinuating that I'm trying to murder the poor thing. It'll turn against me.'

'Actions speak louder than words...' Clemmie ducked back as he turned to fetch the jug, peering out again to see Gil walking back out of the reception area as Maggie waved her hand dismissively at him.

Actions *did* speak louder than words. Gil had told her how much she meant to him, and then his actions had proved him a liar. Clemmie tried to swallow down her anger. The dazzling future she'd imagined for herself had suddenly shrunk into a tremulous hope that she would be able to just get through today. Gil had no right to take away her hopes and dreams, or to damage her career. Taking a deep breath and squaring her shoulders, Clemmie walked back over to the reception desk.

'Gil won't be a minute. He's gone to fetch some water for the plants.' Maggie smiled up at her, then squinted over at the philodendron. 'It looks perfectly fine to me...'

Clemmie turned, surveying the plant. It did look a little sorry for itself, but maybe Gil could sweet-talk it into reviving. Poor thing. Even a plant didn't deserve Gil's brand of loving care...

'He's given me a form for you to fill out. Contact details for while you're here.' Maggie slid a sheet of paper and a pen towards her.

'Right. Thanks.' Clemmie picked up the pen, grateful that she didn't have to talk to Maggie about Gil any more.

She couldn't help glancing up at the corridor that led into the reception area every few seconds, though. If she saw him coming, before he saw her, then maybe it would give her some advantage. Maybe her heart would stop beating so ferociously, and she'd manage to get her knees to stop shaking. Clemmie scribbled down her name and address.

'Here he comes.' Even Maggie's murmured words made her jump. Clemmie forced herself to look up, and saw Gil, exchanging a few words with a cleaner who was working her way along the corridor with a mop.

Don't stare. Clemmie dragged her gaze back to the form in front of her, her mind blank with panic. Telephone number. She wrote the first four digits down and then jumped again as a loud crash sounded from the corridor.

'Oh, for goodness' sake...' Maggie was on her feet, hurrying towards Gil, who was surrounded by water and shards of broken glass. The cleaner was bending to pick up the glass, and Gil stopped her before she cut herself. Maggie began to fuss and was clearly receiving assurances that he was all right. Gil appeared to be attempting to brush the water from his soaked shirt.

She shouldn't laugh. But Gil's obvious embarrassment made her feel a great deal more in charge of the situation. Sometimes, just sometimes, there was a little justice in the world.

Sometimes there wasn't. Gil looked just as delicious wet through as he did dry. More so. He hadn't changed in the last seven years and that male magic was still there, pulling her towards him despite everything she knew and all that she felt.

And... Clemmie looked around. You'd think that in a hospital there would be a doctor or nurse around somewhere, who could rush to his aid. But there was no one, and Gil had snatched his hand from his shirt as a pinkish red stain started to spread across it. Blood could go a very long way when mixed with water, but he'd clearly cut himself. Two of his fingers were curled awkwardly, and Clemmie wondered if he'd done any real damage to his hand.

There was nothing for it. She was going to have to go and check on him. Just standing here, watching a person bleed, wasn't anywhere in her remit as a doctor, and she was a *good* doctor. She'd hung on to that, building her life back up around it.

She heard her heels clack on the floor as she walked towards him. Concentrated on that, and not Gil's sudden stillness when he saw her.

'I'm Dr Clemmie Francis…'

'I know. Gil Alexander.' He held out his hand as if to shake hers and then saw that he had blood on his fingers, from having inspected the cut, and pulled it back again.

'Are you all right?'

He didn't even think about his answer. 'Yeah. I'm fine.'

Take charge. All of Clemmie's professional instincts were screaming at her to do so, and it seemed a good personal strategy, too.

'You're bleeding. Let me take a look.'

'Thanks, but it's nothing. I snagged my hand on some glass.' Gil stepped to one side as the cleaner, armed now with a dustpan and brush, waved him away so she could deal with the mess.

Typical doctor/reluctant patient exchange.

Clemmie could work with that, far better than the conversation that was going on in her head, where she demanded to know why he'd written his number down and begged her to call, when he'd had no intention of ever speaking to her again. There was no possible answer to that question that wouldn't tempt her to slap him.

'The wound needs to be irrigated and dressed.' She looked up at him.

Gil shot her a querying glance. Somewhere, deep in his dark eyes, there was a hint of tenderness that couldn't entirely be accounted for by her offer of medical assistance. Then it was gone. If Gil recognised her, he was clearly keeping quiet about it, which meant that Clemmie could, as well.

'Uh...yeah, thanks. I've got a medical kit in my office.' He turned suddenly, walking briskly along the corridor, and Clemmie followed him.

It was a nice office, light and just tidy enough to inspire confidence. Just messy enough to make someone feel at home. Gil didn't seem over-interested in making Clemmie feel at home, walking directly to the washbasin in one corner and reaching into the cupboard below it to take out a soft bag.

'Let me do that.' Gil was trying to unzip the bag one-handed and Clemmie took it from him. Inside, there were a number of colour-coded bags.

'Blue for cuts.' Gil turned on the cold tap, wincing slightly as he held his hand under the stream of water.

'Can you straighten your fingers for me, please?'

Gil smiled suddenly. 'No. But that's nothing to do with the cut. It's an old injury.' He opened his hand, the little finger staying obstinately curled, and Clemmie watched carefully as he pulled it straight. 'I had a brain bleed, some years ago. I was treated in this hospital.'

So *that* was the reason for Gil's sudden change of course. The last seven years had obviously been no more straightforward for him than they had for Clemmie. And Gil had been the victim of something he couldn't control. Clemmie had made her own mistakes, walking into them with her eyes blurred by tears over him.

She couldn't think about that now. She was having difficulty thinking about *anything* other than that she was too damn close to him and his scent was just the same as it had been before. But inspecting a cut and dressing it were difficult to do at arm's length.

'This hospital?' Clemmie seized on the one

detail that didn't send shock waves hurtling through her.

'Yes. Funny how things turn out, sometimes.'

'Funny?' Clemmie swallowed hard.

'I meant strange…'

Suddenly his gaze caught hers. It still held the silent suggestion that she was the only person within a two-hundred-mile radius that Gil was interested in. Even now, it sent shivers along Clemmie's spine.

It was an effort of will to break away from it and look back down at his hand. For a moment Clemmie could see nothing, and then her medical training came to her rescue. That compartmentalisation that allowed her to set everything else aside and concentrate on a patient.

'I can't see any glass in there…' By some miracle, her tongue was still working and her voice sounded vaguely normal. And she couldn't see any splinters lodged in his palm, which was a relief because Clemmie wasn't sure how she would manage to tweeze shards from a wound while her heart was still beating so fast.

'There's nothing. I had a look myself.'

Clemmie nodded. That was Gil all over—he didn't leave anything to chance. Finding that his control had been wrested from him must have been a cruel blow.

She should stop this. She could feel sympa-

thy for Gil when he wasn't so close, and she
could look at everything more objectively.
Clemmie busied herself with cleaning the cut
and applying three wound-closure strips, then
carefully covering it with a dressing.

But she couldn't help it. She'd fitted everything together so neatly in her head, and now
this. The one piece of information that didn't fit
and was careening around in her brain, tearing
everything else apart. She *had* to ask.

'How long ago was your brain bleed?' She
tried to make the question sound casual, a matter of professional interest.

Gil was silent for a moment, and she glanced
up at him. 'If you don't mind my asking.'

He shook his head. 'Of course not. It'll be
seven years at the end of next month.'

Next month. Clemmie couldn't even work
out what *this* month was at the moment. Today
must be a Monday, because it was her first day
here...

Suddenly she couldn't stay still any longer.
Springing to her feet, she made a grab for her
handbag, and then inspiration hit her.

'I've just remembered... I have to make a
call.' Gil was watching her steadily, his eyebrows slightly raised. 'A patient of mine... I
need to just check on them.'

He nodded. 'Go and do whatever you need

to. I should get changed.' He gestured towards his soaked shirt.

That was the last straw. The thought of Gil unbuttoning his shirt, and the smile that had accompanied it, was altogether too much to bear. Clemmie flung a *thank you* over her shoulder, practically running out of the room.

CHAPTER TWO

GIL SAT MOTIONLESS for a moment, staring after Clemmie. Then he got to his feet, shutting his office door and flipping the lock. The click as the bolt slid home was comforting, even if it was unnecessary.

Everyone knew that when his office door was closed he wasn't to be interrupted. Perhaps the lock was a matter of keeping something in. Now that Clemmie was gone and he had no need to keep them in check, his emotions seemed to be bursting around the room like a tornado, threatening to lay waste to everything in their path.

Clemmie. Her name was Clemmie. Gil allowed himself to savour the name for a moment.

He pulled his wallet out of his back pocket, flipping it open on the desk. His cuff dripped onto the leather and Gil shrugged off his shirt, letting it drop to the floor. One-handed, he fished the photograph carefully from the hidden compartment at the back of the wallet.

It was her. The same dark hair, coiling down around her shoulders, the same oval face and flawless skin. He'd recognised Clemmie as soon as he saw her, and the shock had been so profound that his fingers had tightened around the thin sides of the water jug. It had practically burst in his hands, showering him with glass and water. Everyone had assumed he'd dropped it and it had smashed on the floor, and he hadn't corrected the notion. Clemmie hadn't appeared to recognise him, and he'd allowed that to go unchallenged, as well. He'd thought about this moment for so long, and now it was here he had no idea what to say to her.

Seven years.

It seemed like a whole lifetime ago. To all intents and purposes it was, because he was so different from the man in the photograph, smiling at Clemmie.

Raised in a family of overachievers, Gil had graduated top of his class from medical school and decided that even Australia was too small for him and he wanted the world. Fourteen countries later, he'd come to rest in a busy London A & E department, earning the nickname of 'Stress Eater', because he'd take any amount of pressure without buckling. He'd worked hard and played even harder.

Life had been good. And then he'd woken up in a hospital bed, a stranger amongst strangers.

Slowly he'd begun to reorientate himself. Friends and colleagues had visited, some of whom he'd recognised and some who'd had to remind him who they were. He'd learned how to put a sentence together, and how to hold a cup to his lips when he was thirsty. Taking two steps forward and one back, he'd slowly put the pieces back together again.

But there were still gaps. Some of them inconsequential, and most of them shrinking by the day, but four weeks remained obstinately blank. The two weeks after his injury didn't hold much interest for him, and the nurses who tended him were able to answer all of his questions. The two weeks before were more problematic, largely because there was no one to ask about them.

Gil knew he'd been at a conference, because he remembered packing his case and checking the train times for Manchester. That he must have come back to London on the Saturday, and then gone to play rugby with his club in Richmond on the Sunday. He remembered nothing of that, but his teammates had told him that there had been a collision and that he'd got up and continued playing, seeming none the worse for it. Four hours later, Sam Gordon, one of the surgeons in the neurological unit at Barney's, had found him sitting in the waiting room in A & E, and realised how ill he was. Sam's quick action had probably saved his life.

Then he'd found the photograph in his wallet. He was in a photo booth, sitting close to a beautiful woman, whose face he no longer recognised and whose name he didn't remember. Gil had looked into Clemmie's dark eyes for what felt like the first time, although he knew it couldn't have been. The two of them looked happy, and there was an intimacy there that never failed to send shivers down his spine.

One of the things he'd had to learn was patience. Gil had watched the door, waiting to see if the woman might walk through it at visiting time. It was almost a relief when she didn't because, however much he wanted her smile, he knew that he couldn't compare with the man in the photograph. It had been months before he could pluck up the courage to call the number written on the back of the photograph.

Too long. Gil had been too late. The number was unobtainable, and so was she. She'd stayed that way until this morning, when Clemmie had found her way back into his life. Still as beguiling, but she'd given no clear indication that she recognised him.

Gil pulled some paper towels from the dispenser, shakily dabbing himself dry. Unwrapping the clean shirt he kept in the office, he pulled it across his shoulders, buttoning it clumsily.

He had to get a bit of perspective. He couldn't have known Clemmie for more than a week or so. They must have met at the conference and gone their separate ways. Gil had stared at the photograph, willing himself to remember, so many times that he'd felt he knew the sweet curve of her face better than he knew his own reflection. Clemmie had probably let him go a long time ago, submerged in the sea of faces that she did remember.

He reached for an apple from the bag on his desk. Clemmie had seemed a little jumpy, but who wouldn't in the circumstances? And when he'd responded to her questions, she hadn't taken the bait and searched her memory for him. Maybe he'd lost whatever it was that had ignited the chemistry that the photograph showed so clearly. When she'd looked into his gaze, Gil had thought he felt it again, sizzling between them, but maybe that was just his own reaction and not Clemmie's.

He really wasn't sure that he wanted to know.

right now. Gil had confided all of his hopes and fears to the photograph, and her smile had remained the same, whatever he said. The real Clemmie might not be so accommodating; she had no reason to be. Expecting her to know him, the way he felt he knew her, was ridiculous.

Gil sank his teeth into the apple, reaching for his phone and dialling Reception. When Maggie answered the phone, he could hear a hum of activity in the background.

'I hear you've been patched up. Unlike my jug…' Maggie's no-nonsense approach was like a breath of fresh air.

'Sorry about that, Maggie. I'll get you a new one.'

'That's all right. I have a plastic one at home. I'll bring that in and you can throw it around to your heart's content. Dr Francis has popped out. She said she might be half an hour. She said she had a call to make.' The sound of someone demanding Maggie's attention sounded in the background. 'Right you are. Sorry, Gil, got to go…'

Maggie hung up on him, and Gil sat back in his chair, savouring the taste of the apple. If Clemmie's call was going to last for half an hour that wouldn't be such a bad thing; it would give him time to get his head straight. Fate had given him the chance to get to know the *real* Clemmie, and even though the thought was daunting, it set his pulse racing.

Gil tucked the photograph back into his wallet. If Clemmie didn't remember him, that was probably all for the best. He had the opportunity to forget about the man who'd turned to a photograph for comfort and encouragement, and to start again with a clean slate.

She'd been about to suffocate. Or throw up. Or both. All Clemmie knew was that she had to get away from Gil. She hurried past Reception, remembering to tell Maggie that she'd be back in half an hour, then through the main doors and out into the sunshine. That was no relief at all, because she couldn't run away from herself. But at least she could try to deal with what she'd just heard, without the awkwardness of feeling that her new co-workers might be looking on.

The bench outside the unit was out of the question—far too public. She could go for a coffee in the main hospital building, but she really did feel sick now, and it was always possible that someone from the unit might see her. Clemmie crossed the road, walking into Richmond Park, past the seat she'd sat on this morning to a more secluded one that was shielded from view behind a tree.

Think. *Think!* The conference where she'd met Gil was an annual event, and they must have a website. She took her phone from her pocket, and a search got her to a page that listed out previous conferences and speakers. Tapping on the link for the one that she and Gil had attended, she scanned through for dates.

September the thirteenth to the twenty-seventh. Gil had almost missed his train, because he'd kissed her goodbye one more time at the station. She'd watched him run along the platform and then he'd turned, calling to her that he couldn't wait to speak to her again tomorrow. It was August now and everything fitted. There were only four possible days when he could have sustained the TBI.

Or Gil was lying. He'd recognised her, and had fudged the dates to give himself an excuse for not having called, so that the next six weeks would go a little more smoothly.

The thought was almost comforting. A desperate attempt to hang on to the world as she'd seen it for the last seven years. But there was very little chance that Gil was lying. He was no fool, and it would be easy enough to check the dates in the hospital records. Anyway, who on earth could possibly make this up?

Seven years next month. There had been a vulnerability there when he'd said it, quickly hidden. No one could fake that. Gil wasn't lying and that meant that Clemmie had to adjust her assessment of him. Which meant adjusting a lot of other things, as well.

The thought made her feel physically sick again. Clemmie took a few deep breaths and the hot flush of nausea began to recede. That was a *big* relief. She might not be able to handle what was going on in her head, but at least her body was a little more under control. She sat for a moment, her head in her hands, concentrating on keeping her breathing slow and steady.

What had just happened? She'd found out why a man she'd known for less than a week hadn't picked up the phone, when she'd hoped he would. Seven years ago. That wasn't such a big thing; she should be able to shrug it off by now. Maybe even laugh about it.

But however short-lived their relationship, Gil had been a breath of fresh air. Clemmie had still been living in the shadow of her childhood, when the only person who had seemed to notice her existence was her gran. Then dementia had robbed her grandmother of the ability to notice her, as well. Gil had given her his undivided attention, and, when you added his charm and looks to the mix, it was irresistible.

It had been a whirlwind romance, the love at first sight that she'd never believed happened in real life.

And then he hadn't called. Her calls to him went unanswered. Everything her childhood had taught her, that she was the girl who was unseen and unheard, came back to slap her in the face.

Her broken heart had made mistakes. It had been so easy for her to believe that Gil could just throw her away. Not to expect more from him, because she hadn't thought herself worthy of it. She'd hated Gil, for showing her that life could be different and then taking that all away again.

Clemmie had clung on to what she knew. Married the wrong man and accepted his efforts to belittle and control her for too long before she'd had the self-confidence to break free. She'd concentrated on her career, mending all of the damage that had been done by her turbulent personal life. And now—just as she was getting on her feet again—she'd found that Gil might not have left her after all. That the whole of the last seven years was founded on *her* lie, and not his. The thought brought another wave of nausea, this one stronger than the last.

Deep breaths. Wait until the trembling stops. It wouldn't do to cry here, when some kindly passer-by might see her and stop to ask if she was all right. Clemmie kept her head down, staring at her phone while the cold shivers subsided. Then she blew her nose, wiping her eyes.

A ten-minute walk, brisk enough to get her a little out of breath, was what she needed. Then she could go back inside and face Gil again. Remembering that if what she suspected was true, and she'd been calling his phone while he lay critically ill in hospital, he was the one who was vulnerable.

This was something she could understand. She would have jumped at the chance to help him through the dark days that everyone experienced after a TBI, either as a friend or something more, but he would have had so many other things to think about. Maybe he hadn't felt as much for her as she'd felt for him, but it wasn't a calculated act of rejection.

Time to step up, Clemmie.

She'd found her strength. If Gil didn't recognise her, it would be easy. There was no conflict—she could protect him and herself, along with her career, by never letting him know how much he'd hurt her. She might not be able to change the past, but she could change the future.

CHAPTER THREE

G IL JUMPED FROM the seat behind his desk, ush-
ering Clemmie into his office. She'd walked
for longer than she'd thought, but he didn't ask
where she'd been. He apologised for his clumsy
welcome this morning and waved Clemmie to
a seat, his face betraying nothing.

'Apple?' He pushed the bag on his desk towards her. 'They're home-grown.'

That was unexpected. Gil was the same
in many ways, and that one long look they'd
shared had reminded Clemmie that she wasn't
so different from the young woman who'd
fallen in love with him. But he'd changed, too.

'Um… You grow apples?'

'Yeah. This variety fruits early and I've had
a real glut of them this year.' He smiled suddenly. 'Gardening is my way of winding down.'

Right. The only horticultural aspect of Gil's
so-called winding-down process that Clemmie had been introduced to was strawberries.

With champagne and seduction. On balance, it was probably better to stick to apples. She leaned forward, taking one from the bag and rubbing it against her sleeve. It was shiny and she could smell the apple scent that proved it was home-grown.

'Right, then.' Gil shuffled the papers on his desk. 'Down to business, I suppose. What do you want from your time here with us?'

That was typical of Gil. Asking questions first and listening to the answers. Clemmie avoided his gaze, in case it made her tongue-tied.

'The neurological rehab centre here at Barney's has a reputation for excellence. I want to see all aspects of your work and learn from you.'

'And teach us something?'

Clemmie risked meeting his eyes. 'Learning is always a two-way process.'

He nodded. 'I'm told you're in line to head up your own department at the Royal Victoria Hospital.'

'Nothing's been decided yet. The head of Neurological Rehab there is due to retire at the beginning of next year, and he's hoping for a smooth handover and someone who can build on all the good work he's done. We're working together on a few new initiatives that can be fully developed after he's gone, and…hence my watching brief here.'

Gil's lips curled into a lazy smile. 'In other words, *yes*.'

Clemmie's heart beat a little faster. When they'd last met, he'd told her that she didn't give herself enough credit, and that she shouldn't undersell herself. But now she had the confidence to push back a bit.

'In other words, that's the official position.' Even if Gil was exactly right and she had already been promised the job.

He nodded. 'Well, I'm flattered that you chose to come here.'

Was he fishing for information? Maybe he *did* recognise her, and the idea that he might think she'd come here on purpose rang a shrill alarm in Clemmie's mind.

'My boss suggested it. He was the one who made all of the arrangements.'

Gil didn't miss a beat. 'In that case, we'll have to see if we can justify *his* confidence in us. There are three main aspects to my job…'

He smiled, holding up his hand to count on his fingers. He'd done that once before, when they were discussing one of the conference sessions they'd been to, only he'd counted on her fingers. And the look in his eyes had been so delicious that the only conclusion they'd come to was that work could wait and they wanted to play a little. Clemmie would do well to remember that work was now all-important and play was out of the question.

'First and foremost, as a doctor, I oversee all of our patients' medical needs. There are two other doctors on the unit who work with me, but I have ultimate responsibility for everyone here.'

Clemmie nodded.

'Second… Rehab carries with it a very strong element of motivation, and we're working *with* people in a very real sense. Our counsellor does a great deal in helping patients come to terms with the emotional aspects of what's happening to them, and it's my job to help her to consolidate that.'

'You talk to people.' Clemmie reckoned that Gil's charm helped to inspire no end of confidence.

'In a nutshell, yes. I do a bit more listening than talking, generally. I find I learn a lot more that way. Thirdly, there's the organisational side. It's my job to support all the staff here in being the best they can be. Give them the framework that best allows them to inspire our patients.'

'So you'll be showing me all three of those things?'

Gil nodded. 'Along with anything else you're curious about…?'

Clemmie didn't take the bait. If she'd thought it was hard to be professional with Gil when she hated his guts, now that she'd warmed to him it was letting in all the old memories. She had to be careful.

Gil paused, waiting for her answer, and then shrugged.

'Right, then. We also value our close links with the surgical unit, over in the main building, in terms of continuity of care. Sam Gordon's a neurological surgeon and I usually meet with her for lunch at least once a week, as well as liaising with her closely on a day-to-day basis, but she's on maternity leave at the moment. Maybe we can organise a lunch meeting sometime in the next few weeks. I'm sure it would be helpful for you to have a chat with her.'

'I don't want to break in on her maternity leave…' Gil's eyes had softened momentarily, and it occurred to Clemmie that this Sam Gordon might be his partner. That the baby might be his… She tried to clear the lump that had formed in her throat.

'That's okay. I mentioned it to her the other day and she'd be very happy to see you. She's already interrogating me about how things are going at work whenever I see her. I dare say you'll bump into her fiancé at some point. Yanis is also a neurological surgeon. Sam's just had twin girls, and it'll be a great excuse for me to play godfather while you two talk business.'

Perfect. Trying to concentrate on holding a sensible conversation, while Gil was playing with two newborns. Clemmie had once dared to imagine a future in which he might be the father of the children that she so wanted. That she *had* so wanted, before life had set in and destroyed her confidence in ever being able to make a good relationship with someone she loved. But the instinctive tug still pulled at her.

But she'd made up her mind not to show any fear. She could watch Gil holding a baby and come out of it unscathed.

'That would be very helpful. Thank you.'

Gil nodded, turning his attention to his phone, which had started to vibrate urgently on his desk. He glanced at a message, and suddenly his relaxed demeanour changed.

This was the Gil that Clemmie knew. The gleam in his eyes as a challenge presented itself. Ready to face anything.

'Someone's fallen.' He didn't waste words, turning to the glazed double doors behind his desk, which looked out into a garden behind the unit. He opened them, moving outside swiftly.

Clemmie got to her feet and followed. Participating in conference sessions with him had made it clear that Gil was an excellent doctor, and the kind of person that everyone wanted around in an emergency, but she'd never seen him deal with a real situation. This was the aspect of his job that she was the most curious about.

He was hurrying across the lawn, towards a group of greenhouses, and Clemmie caught him up at the door of one of them. He quickly ushered her inside. Between the long row of benches, covered with trays of green seedlings, she saw an elderly woman lying on the ground, a young woman in a nurse's tunic beside her, holding her hand and urging her to stay still.

'Elaine…?'

The nurse looked up at him. 'Jeannie slid off her seat. I didn't see her hit her head…'

'I think I could get up now, if someone would just give me a hand. There's no need for all this fuss.' The elderly woman frowned up at Gil and he smiled, squatting down beside her.

'We can't be too careful, Jeannie. Elaine did exactly the right thing in asking you to stay right where you were until I got here.' Gil glanced at Elaine, nodding his approval, and some of the tension lifted from her face.

He was good. Very thorough. He examined

Jeannie's head and neck, carefully gauging her reactions and level of alertness. Gil's serious intent was masked by relaxed jokes and encouragement for Jeannie.

'This is Clemmie.' He introduced her as he worked. 'She's a doctor and attached to the unit for six weeks, and so you'll be seeing her around a bit. She may be wanting a chat to see what you think of the place.'

'Oh. And I suppose you'll be wanting me to give you a good report.' Jeannie was quite clearly a match for anyone, including Gil.

'Of course I do. But I'll settle for firm but fair.' Gil's attention had moved to Jeannie's hip and legs, to check there was no injury there. 'Does that hurt at all?'

'No.' Jeannie shot him an impatient look, and then turned her gaze onto Clemmie. 'Now, don't you take any old nonsense from him, will you?'

Best advice she'd had all morning. The more she found to forgive, the more difficult it was to resist Gil's charm.

'Thanks. I won't.'

Gil finished his examination and sat back on his heels. 'Since I've failed to find anything wrong with you, I think we'd best get you on your feet, eh, Jeannie? Elaine, can you bring the wheelchair over, please? And call someone to take Jeannie back to her room, as well.'

'About time. I'll be late for tea if you don't hurry up.'

'You'll get your tea, even if I have to make it myself.' Gil grinned.

'I don't think I'd want you to do *that*.' Jeannie's teasing was clearly the result of liking Gil a lot, the kind of easy doctor-patient relationship that all good practitioners tried to cultivate.

'Clemmie…?' Gil turned to her. Elaine was a member of staff, and the obvious person to ask for help in lifting Jeannie, but the girl seemed very shaken by what had happened. Clemmie nodded.

His eyes, again. Checking that they were both balanced and ready to lift Jeannie upright. Clemmie felt herself flush, and ignored the touch of his fingers behind Jeannie's shoulders. On his count, they lifted her smoothly to her feet and then into the wheelchair that Elaine had positioned next to them.

'See you later, Jeannie.' Gil gave her a smile as another nurse arrived to take Jeannie back inside.

'Don't fuss…'

'It's my job. I get paid extra for fussing,' Gil

retorted. Jeannie flapped her hand dismissively as she was wheeled away.

'Elaine...' Gil quietly stopped her from following.

'I'm so sorry.' Elaine was obviously blaming herself for the fall. 'I'd followed all the guidance, but I turned away for one minute to fetch something for her, and she just slid out of the chair.'

'It's okay,' Gil reassured her. 'We'll need to make out a patient incident report, but what I want you to remember is that the aim of it is to improve patient safety, not find someone to blame. They help me to do my job better.'

Elaine nodded, biting her lip.

'Go and ask Maggie if she'll give you a form, write everything down straight away while it's fresh in your mind and then come and see me this afternoon so we can have a chat about it. And don't look so worried, eh?'

'Okay. Thanks.' Elaine gave him a relieved smile and hurried away.

Gil stood silently, watching her go. It was a difficult balance; his patients' needs were paramount, but at the same time he must support his staff. Clemmie would need to consider that same balance if she took on the running of her own unit.

'What happens next?'

Gil pressed his lips together, turning to pick up one of the plant trays that had fallen onto the floor, and collecting the seedlings that had been uprooted. Carefully smoothing the soil and replanting them seemed to figure somewhere in his thought process.

'Accidents happen—we'll never be able to prevent that. Elaine's very new, but from what I've seen of her, she's very conscientious about safety and patient care. We have to discuss what happened honestly, and look to correct any mistakes that were made. And reassure Elaine about the things she couldn't have prevented. She seems pretty eager to shoulder all of the responsibility for this.'

Clemmie nodded. 'And Jeannie?'

'The nurses will keep a close eye on her. I'll let her have her tea and then go and have a word, get her version of what happened. Confidence is always an important issue to address, after any fall.' He smoothed the earth around the seedlings carefully, making sure they were all upright. 'Have I missed anything?'

'No, I don't think so.' His approach was fair and constructive. Clemmie bent down to pick up a small plant that was still on the ground. 'Apart from this.'

His fingers touched her palm as he picked the plant up, and Clemmie shivered, even at this momentary contact. Gil replanted the seedling, and then brushed the soil from his fingers.

'That'll do for now...' He reached for a broom, clearing the scattered earth from the walkway and setting the chair that Jeannie had been sitting on back on its feet, checking that it was stable. Moving slowly and deliberately, as if still deep in thought.

'This flooring...?' Clemmie reckoned that the slight give in the tiles that covered the floor in the greenhouse would have cushioned Jeannie's fall.

Gil smiled suddenly. 'You noticed. The tiles are made of a rubber compound similar to what's used in children's playgrounds. They're non-slip, and if anyone does fall, they make for a softer landing. We keep everything tidy in here, and try to eliminate hard corners.' He ran his hand along the rubber lip that was fixed along the edges of the bench.

'It's impressive. I'll be wanting to take another look in here.' Everything was well organised and done with care. Colourful too, the space bright and attractive.

'Be my guest. We're lucky to have this space. Gardening's the most popular of all our therapies. And the garden's nice for patients to come and sit outside, as well.'

'A larger area for you to monitor.'

Gil grinned suddenly. That delicious, loving-the-challenge smile. 'Yeah. It would be a great deal easier to make them all stay in their beds. That's not really what we're here for, is it? Our job is all about widening people's horizons.'

That was exactly how Clemmie saw it. She confined herself to a brief nod and followed Gil out of the greenhouse.

It had seemed like a long day, although in truth it had been only nine to five. But it had been eight hours of intense concentration, trying to analyse Clemmie's every word. Her every move. Sometimes Gil thought he saw recognition in her eyes, and sometimes not.

He'd left her to her own devices while he went to see Jeannie, and then given her the standard tour of the unit, introducing her to everyone. Clemmie had accompanied him on his afternoon rounds, and he'd watched her carefully. She was great with his patients, confident and friendly, listening to what they had to say as if she had all the time in the world. No wonder she was on a fast track to promotion—she seemed to have all the skills that were required to run her own unit. All she needed was a little more experience.

Gil wished her a good evening and went back to his office, puffing out a breath. When he took the photograph out of his wallet again, he could better understand the look on his face as he stared at Clemmie. She wasn't just beautiful. She was clever and kind and had all of the qualities that would make a man want to sit and listen to her, all evening and late into the night.

He propped the photo up against the phone, leaning back in his seat and putting his feet up on the desk. It seemed that much more precious to him now, but he still couldn't fathom a way of asking Clemmie if she remembered having met him before. It was a risky excursion into the unknown, and if Clemmie *did* remember and was keeping quiet about it, then that raised all kinds of awkward questions.

A knock sounded on his door and he looked up. Anya Whitehead breezed into his office, a gauzy purple scarf trailing in her wake.

'You called?'

Gil smiled. 'And you came.'

'Of course I did. You're looking very deep in thought.' Anya fixed him with one of those searching, perceptive looks that she was so good at.

He'd met Anya when he was a patient here, after his own brain injury. She'd been assigned as his counsellor and had done everything to encourage him to talk, despite Gil's dogged resistance. They'd come to an understanding, Gil acknowledging that he had difficulty in admitting that he *had* any problems, and Anya challenging him to go away and think about that. When Gil had started to recover, and was considering the idea that maybe his future career lay in Rehab rather than emergency medicine, Anya's listening ear had helped him make the right decision.

'I'm just considering a few awkward questions.' Gil grinned at her, taking his feet off the desk and flipping the photograph face down.

'Goody. You know I like awkward questions.' Anya sat down.

'It's nothing…' Gil shrugged. It wasn't nothing, but if he had something to say, he should say it to Clemmie first.

'Of course it is. Well, you know where Miss Purple is when you want her.'

Gil chuckled. When he'd first known Anya, he'd still been struggling with expressive aphasia and the simplest words would elude him. Names were a particular problem, and he'd called Anya 'Miss Purple' because it was unusual for her not to include the colour somewhere in her outfit. It had become a standing joke between them.

'What I'd really like is if you could spare some time to talk to the doctor I'm working with at the moment, Clemmie Francis. She's here for six weeks, to see how we do things, and it would be great if you could give her an overview of your work in the unit.'

'Ah yes, I'd heard you had a visitor. Of course. Give her my number and we can sort out a time.' Anya gave him another searching look. 'Anything else?'

Gil knew that ruse, and he wasn't going to fall for it.

'I don't think so. Want an apple?' He pushed the bag towards her.

'Can I take two? My kids love these. They're so sweet.'

'Take the bag. Please. I have a lot more at home.'

'Thank you. Oh, and by the way, Jamie's bike's back from the repair shop, so he's up for Sunday if you're not too busy.' Gil and Anya's husband often met on Sundays for an early morning ride around Richmond Park.

'Sure, I'll give him a call. Anything else?' Gil pulled a face to exaggerate the joke.

'Hm. I'm sure there must be. Your fingers don't lie, Gil.' Anya nodded to his hand and Gil realised that he'd been massaging his curled fingers. It had been a stress reaction, constantly massaging his fingers and arm in the hope that they might respond a little quicker, and he and

Anya had talked about it when he was a patient here. He hadn't done it in years.

'I cut my hand.' And he'd met Clemmie.

Anya knew it was an excuse, and let him get away with it, because she and Gil had fought that battle before, and she knew he wouldn't talk about things he didn't want to. She gathered up the apples and got to her feet.

'Okay. Don't stay too late, will you? I dare say the awkward questions will manage on their own for a little while—they don't need your constant supervision.'

'You mean the world's not going to collapse if I take my eye off it for a moment?' He shot Anya a look of mock horror and she laughed.

'Go home and pick me some more apples. Smell a few flowers while you're at it, Gil.'

It wasn't a bad idea. Gil supposed he'd reverted to the old habit of massaging his fingers because Clemmie's arrival had brought back the last piece of unfinished business from his brain injury so vividly. Or maybe it was just that he felt so confused about this situation, the way he'd felt back then.

But he had a few things to do still, if he was going to have time available for Clemmie tomorrow. And his determination to make the day run more smoothly than today had done was all he had in the way of control over what happened next.

He couldn't let this break him, the way he'd been broken before. And he wouldn't allow his own feelings to complicate matters. Gil heaved a sigh, picking the photograph up from his desk and putting it back out of sight in his wallet.

Clemmie had made the long journey home, through the evening rush hour. Dropping her bag in the hall, she made a cup of tea and then threw herself down on the sofa. Today hadn't gone entirely as planned, but then, who could possibly have planned for something like this?

Gil was doing it all over again. No…actually *she* was doing it again. Liking him. Wanting to hear his opinion. Watching the way he moved, which only brought tantalising flashbacks of how she had once responded to his caress. It was beyond unacceptable.

Gil was a little different from the way she remembered him. More measured and thoughtful, not quite so keen to squeeze everything from the moment. Maybe that was because this time she was working with him, rather than indulging in a whirlwind of romantic gestures, which inevitably led to wild and wonderful sex.

She couldn't imagine that the Gil she'd known would bring a bag of home-grown apples to work, or stop to rescue seedlings that had been tipped onto the ground. But he was still the kind of man that any woman could make a fool of herself with. That Clemmie *had* made a fool of herself with. It wasn't enough to simply accept that she'd been wrong in thinking so badly of Gil and then move on. She had to protect herself, and him, too.

She reached for the tapestry cushion that sat beside her on the sofa, hugging it tightly. It was about the only thing she had left of her grandmother, and Clemmie really needed her now.

She'd spent most of her time at her gran's house when she was little. Her parents had worked hard, and never had much time to spend with their daughter, but that had never mattered to Clemmie because Gran was there. Until the unrelenting slide into dementia had taken her away.

Her gran had gone into a nursing home when Clemmie was thirteen, and the loss of the only place that had ever really felt like home was profound. She visited every afternoon, after school, watching the light slowly fade from her grandmother's eyes. Time took its toll, and when her grandmother had died, she hadn't known that the young medical student, sitting by her bed and holding her hand, had been her granddaughter.

In the years that followed, Clemmie had felt herself disappearing, with no one left who would see or hear her. Gil had shown her that she could no longer live in the shadows, and then he'd been taken from her. There was no way back now; too much had happened in her life and she couldn't just flip a switch and make it un-happen. And Gil couldn't know how much she'd invested in their brief relationship. He'd had every reason not to call her, but the Gil she knew hadn't cut himself a great deal of slack and probably wouldn't see it that way.

And Gil was still dangerous. Every time she saw him she felt herself falling under his spell again. Wanting him even more than she had before, because now she knew how hard-won his success was. He'd been crushed, and he'd built his life back up again, piece by piece.

There was only one thing for it. She'd take a leaf from Gil's book—the old Gil—and squeeze every professional opportunity she could from the next six weeks. And then she'd leave. She wouldn't look back and he'd never know just how special he'd been to her.

CHAPTER FOUR

THE MAN WHO held the door open for her to enter the rehab unit the following morning had an unmistakable spring in his step. As Clemmie stopped to greet Maggie, she saw Gil hurrying out to meet him.

'Yanis…' Gil shook his hand vigorously. 'What are you doing here? Tired of waiting on Sam?'

Yanis grinned. A bright smile that said life was treating him well. 'I'm never tired of that. She insisted I come into work this morning.'

'She must be feeling better, then. And how are the twins?'

'Beautiful.' Yanis's French accent made the word sound special. 'Sam heard that one of her patients was coming over to Rehab from the surgical unit, and sent me to make sure the handover went smoothly.'

Gil chuckled. 'I'm surprised she didn't demand you brought her over here to do it her-self.'

'She tried.' Yanis gave a smiling shrug and his blue eyes sparkled. 'I promised her I'd ask you over to dinner tonight and I'm under in-structions not to take *no* for an answer.'

'That'll be a *yes*, then, thank you. I haven't had my fill of baby-holding yet. I'll bring some fresh-picked strawberries...'

The two men were still talking, but the image of strawberries and champagne was blocking everything else out. How did that work, that four short days and three long nights could overshadow everything else so completely?

Clemmie wondered if she should slip past the two men and find something else to do, until Gil was free to chat about the sessions he'd promised to arrange with all the key workers in the unit. But Gil had seen her now, and he and Yanis were walking towards her.

'Clemmie, this is Yanis Baptiste. I mentioned Sam Gordon to you yesterday, and Yanis is her fiancé. He works over in the main hospital in the surgical neurology department.'

Clemmie turned to Yanis, feeling her shoul-ders relax. He was handsome, the blue spar-kle in his eyes evidence that Sam Gordon was a lucky woman. But that was all it was—evidence. Something she could think about rationally without feeling every nerve ending explode the way they did when she looked at Gil.

'Pleased to meet you.'

Yanis nodded, shaking her hand. Not a trace of the inappropriate electricity that had sparked in response to Gil's handshake yesterday.

'I'm standing in for Sam at the moment.' Yanis grinned brightly. 'Have you heard that we've just had twins?'

Gil chuckled quietly. 'If there's anyone in Richmond you *haven't* told yet, I'll help you get round to them this evening...'

Yanis was laughing, and Clemmie kept her gaze studiedly on him, ignoring Gil. 'That's news worth sharing. Congratulations to both of you. Do you have a photograph?'

Yanis took his phone from his pocket, swiping through images and then handing it to Clemmie. At the mention of photographs, Maggie shot to her feet, rounding the reception desk with breakneck speed.

'You walked straight past me with *photographs* in your pocket, Yanis? How *could* you?' Maggie leaned in close to Clemmie, and she held the phone between them, flipping slowly through the pictures.

A woman with red hair, her face aglow. Clearly Yanis had been spending most of his time recently capturing as many images as possible of his partner and their two tiny babies. It was heart-warming. An echo of what Clemmie had wanted for herself, before she'd realised that finding herself meant being alone.

'Gorgeous!' Maggie delivered the smiling assessment that Clemmie probably should have voiced. 'Anna, come here. Yanis has photographs.'

The young nurse who was passing through Reception stopped suddenly and hurried over, craning to see the pictures over Clemmie's other shoulder. This was nice. Being part of something that was full of warmth and happiness and didn't focus on Gil.

But out of the corner of her eye, she could see Gil and Yanis discussing something. Probably to do with their new patient, and Clemmie really ought to be a part of that. Reluctantly she handed the phone over to Maggie, and joined the two men.

'Your photographs are wonderful, Yanis, thank you.'

Yanis nodded, smiling. 'I'm actually here to deliver some notes. I'll be bringing your latest patient over in a moment. It's one of Sam and Gil's little traditions. Sam's there to say goodbye and Gil's waiting to welcome them.'

'It's a good idea. I imagine it makes the transfer much less stressful for your patients.' Clemmie addressed Yanis, ignoring Gil completely.

'Yes, it does. It's one of the things that impressed me when I first came here.' Yanis seemed just as determined to include Gil as Clemmie was to exclude him. 'Both Sam and Gil have busy schedules, but they try to make time for the little things, too.'

'Now you mention little things... I'm just going to check on the room we have ready. Perhaps you'd like to go with Yanis?' Gil avoided Clemmie's gaze, even though his question was clearly aimed at her.

'If that's okay...?' Clemmie directed hers in Yanis's direction.

'Yes, of course. As soon as I can get my phone back...'

Yanis had managed to wrest his phone from Maggie's grip by promising she could have it back again later. Clemmie walked beside him, over to the main hospital building, feeling a little calmer now that she was out of Gil's range. For the moment, he could get on with whatever he was supposed to do, and she could spend her time doing what she was supposed to do, watching and learning.

The building was even more impressive inside than it was from the outside. Not just clean and functional, it was built to include soaring spaces and light, too. A place to lift the spirits, as well as meet patients' medical needs. As Yanis led her through the atrium, Clemmie couldn't help glancing up towards the glass ceiling, eight floors above her head, and he stopped for a moment so she could take in her surroundings. The greenery, twisting walkways and benches lent a sense of peace to the space, even though it was right at the heart of a busy hospital. This was somewhere that staff and visitors alike could catch their breath. At either side were slender-trunked giant ficus trees in huge containers, their spreading canopies reaching up into the atrium and providing dappled shade for those who sat beneath them.

'This is just as important as the technology we have here,' he murmured quietly. 'In a different way.'

Clemmie nodded. 'Yes. The Royal Victoria is really nice, and everyone does their best to make it welcoming, but this place is…something different altogether.'

Yanis led the way to the lift, and then back out into Neurosurgery. When he ushered her into a private room, it seemed that their patient was all ready to go. A nurse was helping a young girl into a wheelchair, talking to her as she did so.

'This is Jahira.' Yanis smiled at the teenager. 'Jahira, this is Clemmie. She's one of the doctors who'll be looking after you at the rehab centre.'

Jahira eyed Clemmie silently. There was a trace of caution in her face, which was only to be expected, and Clemmie stepped forward.

'Hi, Jahira. We're looking forward to getting to know you.'

'Thanks.'

One word, but Jahira had clearly been through a bad time already, and her wariness was more than understandable. The left side of her head had been shaved, and her dark hair was swept over to one side of her face, flat and lifeless. One hand lay in her lap, and she was massaging her fingers with the other hand, as if she needed urgently to bring them back to full working order. Clemmie realised that she'd seen Gil display that same stress reaction yesterday.

'Your mum and dad will be coming soon. They'll help you settle in.' Yanis added the information.

'They know where to find me?' Jahira's speech was a little slurred and panic showed suddenly in her eyes. 'Cos I don't know where I'm going...'

'They know exactly where to find you. Your mum's been over there already, to check on

your room and bring some of your clothes,'
Yanis reassured her.

'Uh... Maybe she said...' Jahira shook her
head.

This was hard for Jahira. Out of control, re-
lying on other people for everything. Clemmie had seen this so many times before. Yanis
seemed to be in no rush, and she sat down in
the chair beside Jahira's bed.

'Before we go, is there anything you'd like
to do here?'

'Sarah. Does *she* know how to find me?'

Clemmie glanced over her shoulder at Yanis,
who nodded towards a brightly coloured card
that stood on the cabinet next to the bed. She
reached for it, handing it over to Jahira.

'Is this from Sarah?'

Jahira nodded, opening the card and staring
at the rounded writing inside.

'It's a lovely card. What does it say?' Clemmie waited, giving Jahira some time to focus.

'She says she's coming to see me. In Rehab.'

'That's really nice. I'll bet you've been missing everyone. Sarah sounds really special.'

Jahira nodded. Her eyes were still on the
card, and Clemmie took it from her hands,
tucking it into the blanket across Jahira's legs.
'You'd better take good care of this—you don't

want to lose it. Is there anything else you need to bring?'

'My photographs…' Jahira looked around the room and Yanis gestured towards a bag that lay at the end of the bed.

'We packed those already, along with your other things.'

'You're sure?' Jahira frowned and Yanis bent down, unzipping the bag and taking out a photo cube. Jahira reached for it.

There was a photo of her with another girl, their arms around each other. One of Jahira with two dogs, and another of a man and woman together, who must be her parents. She looked at each one, turning the cube awkwardly in her hand, her fingers stroking the smiling faces in an expression of longing that tore at Clemmie's heart.

'Yeah. This is right.' Jahira looked up.

'Would you like me to take care of that for you?' Clemmie volunteered. 'It'll be the first thing we find a place for in your new room.'

'Yes, please.' Jahira gave Clemmie the cube, and Yanis zipped up her bag, looping the straps over his shoulder.

'Ready to go?'

'What happens if I don't like it?' Panic flared again in Jahira's eyes.

Yanis grinned. 'You like it here?'

Jahira looked around. 'No. Not really. It's nice and everything but...'

'It's not home, is it?' Yanis clearly understood where Jahira really wanted to be. 'But the rooms at the rehab unit are much nicer. You'll be able to have things the way you like them and a few more visitors. After that you'll be going home. How does that sound?'

Jahira sighed, clearly resigning herself to the inevitable. 'Yeah. Sounds okay.'

Yanis had pushed the wheelchair, taking his time and stopping to let Jahira say her goodbyes to the staff in the surgical unit. Clemmie had carried the photo cube, making sure that Jahira could see that it wasn't being left behind. When they entered the rehab unit, Gil was waiting in the reception area.

'Hi. You're Jahira? My name's Gil.'

'Gil...' Jahira stared at him, clearly making an effort to connect the name with the face. 'What do you do?'

'I'm a doctor, so you'll see me every day. I'm also in charge here, so if there's anything you're unhappy about then I want you to tell me about it, and I'll do my best to fix things for you.'

Jahira nodded thoughtfully. Gil was reaching out, trying to get through to her, and he was saying all the right things. He'd just given

Jahira a hotline to the man in charge, and that was important for someone who felt unsure and out of control.

'My photos. And my card...' Jahira pulled the card out from under the blanket.

'You're going to need somewhere safe for those. Come with me and we'll fix that up straight away.'

Gil clearly knew how important those little things were to Jahira, and that they connected her to her home and the people she loved. He straightened up, waiting while Yanis said his goodbyes, and then wheeled the chair out of the reception area and along a corridor. One of the doors at the far end was open, and Clemmie followed them inside.

Jahira silently looked around the room. The rooms here still had the trappings of a hospital, a hospital bed and a power-assisted easy chair. But every effort had been made to make them homely, with curtains at the window, a wardrobe and a small writing table. And there was a bright bedspread on the bed, with some cushions that Jahira's mother had obviously brought from home.

'Hot in here...'

'Yeah, you're right.' Gil strode over to the window, opening it. 'Better?'

Jahira nodded.

'What about your card, and your photos? Where would you like those?'

'There.' Jahira pointed towards the cabinet next to the bed and then handed her card to Clemmie, who arranged the photo cube and card so that they could be seen from the bed and the easy chair. Clemmie then turned to Jahira.

'How's that?'

'Yes. Thank you.'

'Would you like to try the chair out?' Gil motioned towards the easy chair.

'My gran's got one like that.' Jahira turned the edges of her mouth down. 'It helps her get up.'

'Yeah?' Gil grinned. 'Well, I guess you'll know what to do with the controls, then. It's not going to be for ever, just to help you for a little while.'

Jahira's hand gripped one of the armrests of the wheelchair, and her dark eyes filled with tears. Clumsily she tried to wipe them away with her other hand. Clemmie moved to comfort her but Gil was already there, pulling the chair that was tucked under the desk around to face Jahira and sitting down on it.

'What's up?'

'You're going to fix it?' Jahira's question sounded a lot like a challenge. Always a red rag to a bull where Gil was concerned. Clemmie froze as the memories of all the challenges she'd thrown at him, and which he'd met so deliciously, assailed her yet again.

'There are some things I can't fix. But if I can, I will fix it for you. Try me.'

'Want to go *home*.' Tears started to course down Jahira's cheeks.

'I want you to go home, too. I don't want you here.' Gil handed her a tissue, waiting for his words to sink in. When they did, Jahira stared at him uncomprehendingly.

'Here's the thing. You're going to leave that wheelchair behind and walk out of here yourself. Reach out with that arm…' Gil motioned towards Jahira's left arm, which lay uselessly in her lap '…open the door and go.'

This was tough love. And it was risky. Clemmie felt the back of her neck prickle with alarm.

'I'll do it at home… The…things… Exercises.' Jahira was pleading with him now, and the look in her eyes was enough to melt anyone's heart.

'Maybe you would. I can help you recover better and faster, though. We'll be asking a lot of you here, and sometimes you won't see the point of it. But it works.'

'You don't *know*…' Jahira's lip curled. Maybe an attempt to smile, but from the scorn in her eyes, Clemmie didn't think so. She hoped that Gil knew what he was doing, because he seemed to be pushing Jahira awfully hard.

'I know that you're scared, and wondering if anything's ever going to be the same again. You're busy pretending that everything's all right, but really you just want to run.'

Gil's voice was tender, and Jahira was staring silently at him now. He was getting through to her.

'I've done this before. I know I can help you to run if you'll let me. Your mum tells me that you want to go to veterinary college. I'd like to help you make that happen, too.'

Silence. 'Do we have a deal, Jahira? You don't have to like it, and you probably won't like me too much when I ask you to do things that you think you can't. But I promise I'm not going to give up on you.'

Jahira nodded. 'Okay. Deal.'

Gil smiled. 'All right. What's next, then? The first thing on your list of things to do, to get you on the road home and then off to veterinary college.'

Jahira looked around the room. 'My stuff.' She nodded towards the bag of belongings they'd brought with them.

'Sounds good. Your mum will be here soon. Would you like me to send one of the nurses to unpack your things so you can be settled in when she gets here?'

'I'll stay.' Clemmie broke in quickly. Gil had obviously decided that Jahira had taken about as much challenge as she could manage right now, and that he should leave her alone to settle. Clemmie could do with some time away from Gil, as well. 'If you'd like, I can help you arrange everything the way you want it, Jahira.'

'Yes. Thanks.'

Gil's gaze flipped towards Clemmie for a moment, and then he stood.

'Okay. I'll leave you to get on with that, then.' He pointed to the call button, which lay on the bed. 'There's your hotline, Jahira. Make sure you use it if there's something you need.'

He'd done a good job. Clemmie knew that feeling helpless and unable to communicate was common in patients with traumatic brain injuries, and Gil had given Jahira some much-needed control. She wasn't going to think about how he'd managed to get inside her head, or whether Jahira's reaction to him was because she saw that he understood. Clemmie was here to learn, and part of the learning curve was going to be resisting the temptation to fall for Gil all over again.

Gil helped Jahira take a few slow, hesitant steps, and settled her into the armchair. Then he folded the wheelchair, taking it with him when he left. Clemmie lifted Jahira's bag, putting it on the floor at her feet, and bent down to unzip it.

'Right, then. What goes where?'

Gil walked back to his office, flexing his fingers. Clemmie was doing exactly as he'd wanted her to do, getting involved and using her own expertise to become a part of the process here and see how it worked. He wasn't as pleased about that as he'd wanted to be.

He'd decided to keep the photograph under wraps today, and stop staring at it so obsessively. But before he could stop himself, he'd taken it out of his wallet and propped it back up against the phone.

How could anyone look at someone the way that Clemmie was looking at him, and then forget all about them? Gil had gone over it time and time again, trying to recall people he'd met seven years ago. There were the blanks, caused by the brain injury, but apart from that, he didn't think that anyone had just dropped out of his head like that.

But he'd had the photograph. It had been something more than just an enigma. It reminded him of his past, the ways in which he'd changed, and the ways in which he was the same. He was still ambitious and still wanted to be the best at what he did. He'd just learned to deal with that in different ways.

Stop and smell the flowers.

It was ironic that this had literally become one of his ways of coping. The slow process of preparing the ground and watching things grow had started here, when he'd managed to beg some tools from one of the hospital's gardeners and gone out to attack a piece of rough ground. It had been a difficult, painstaking process, and he'd fallen more than once. Clawed at the earth, raging at his own inability to transform it as quickly as he wanted to.

But the staff had stood back and let him do it. Allowed him to push himself to the limit and take out his frustrations on Mother Nature. And he'd learned to love it, to take sustenance from the slow pace and pride in the new green shoots he had nurtured.

And now Clemmie. The woman he'd been afraid to call, because he'd been raging against his own weaknesses. When he'd finally plucked up the courage, it had been too late. When he thought about it now, he wasn't even sure he wanted her to recognise him. He'd worked so hard to leave the man that he was then behind. Even if he couldn't help looking at her now and hoping she'd remember that wide-eyed expression she had on her face in the photograph.

'Stop it.' He muttered the words to himself under his breath. It was seeming more and more likely that Clemmie didn't *want* to remember and he had to respect that. Do what he could to make these next six weeks work for her, and then learn to say goodbye to the image that had sustained him and kept him honest for the last seven years.

Gil was only just beginning to understand how hard that was going to be.

CHAPTER FIVE

CLEMMIE HAD SPENT time arranging all of Jahira's belongings, plumping the cushions and folding the bedspread just the way Jahira liked it. When her parents arrived, they found their daughter bubbling with excitement and wanting to explore the rest of the unit with them. Clemmie fetched a wheelchair, settling Jahira into it, and left them to it.

Gil had lost no time in fulfilling his promise to set up sessions with the therapists who worked in the rehab unit, and Maggie had several messages for her. Anya Whitehead, one of the hospital counsellors who took care of the unit's patients, had some free time this afternoon and Gil was nowhere to be found, so Clemmie left a message on his desk telling him where she was, and walked over to Anya's office in the main hospital building.

Her own work had taught her the importance of counselling, but here the service seemed more integrated with the other therapies the unit offered. Anya spoke about the many and different issues that patients in the neurology units faced, and then went on to talk about the way she'd worked with Gil to help make a supportive environment for his patients.

'From what I've seen, he seems to understand what's needed, very well.' Clemmie supposed that the compliment was okay, since Gil wasn't actually around to hear it.

'Yes, he does.' Anya smiled. 'There's something to be said for having seen both sides of the process.'

'Gil said he'd suffered a traumatic brain injury himself. I imagine that must help him a lot in his work.'

Anya pressed her lips together. 'Yes and no. Gil has an extraordinary way of empathising with his patients, but I'm sure you're aware of how difficult it is to recover completely from a traumatic brain injury.'

'He mentioned his fingers.' Despite herself, Clemmie was seized with a wish to know more.

'Yes. I'm thinking more about the psychological effects.' Anya shot her a thoughtful look. 'Gil makes no secret of it—everyone here knows what happened to him. He suffers from retrograde amnesia.'

What? Clemmie felt herself stiffen. Generally speaking, if retrograde amnesia was present, it covered a time period immediately before an injury.

'Retrograde amnesia is something that particularly interests me. I've seen it in some of my patients.' Clemmie neglected to mention that the thing about Gil's retrograde amnesia that really interested her was whether it covered the two weeks at the conference they'd both attended.

'Yes, it's an interesting phenomenon. You should definitely ask Gil about it. He always says that it was one of the more difficult things to come to terms with.' Anya smiled. 'I'll leave him to tell you about our little struggles over it.'

'You were his counsellor?' Clemmie could imagine that there *were* struggles. The Gil she'd known didn't seem very good at biding his time and staying within his limits. He'd taken her way beyond *her* limits...

'Yes. He's usually generous enough to say that he learned a lot from me, but I actually learned a great deal from him.'

Mutual respect. Learning a lot. This was getting more interesting by the minute. But it wasn't really fair to ask Anya about it; she had her own confidentiality to maintain. She'd told Clemmie the things that Gil had obviously made clear were for public consumption, but asking any more of her would be wrong.

She had to know, though. And somehow she had to find out without betraying too much to Gil. If he didn't remember her then it was best to let sleeping dogs lie. Her placement here meant a lot to her, and the last time she'd got involved with Gil on a personal basis, her work had suffered. She couldn't let that happen again.

'I'll bear that in mind when I ask him.' Clemmie took a deep breath, wondering how on earth she was going to broach the subject.

'Do.' Anya looked at her watch. 'I have a patient in half an hour. Have you been to our wonderful coffee bar yet?'

'No, I haven't had the chance. I must make the time to take a look around here. It seems like a very well-thought-out building.'

'It is.' Anya got to her feet. 'I'm very interested in the role of environment in healing—it's something Gil and I have endless discussions about. Let me buy you a coffee and we'll appreciate the architecture together...'

Knowing that Clemmie was in the main building with Anya had allowed Gil a moment to breathe. He had shoehorned himself back into his usual routine, and that was surprisingly restful, as well.

And then, just when he thought it was probably time for her to go home, and he wouldn't see her again today, Clemmie walked into his office. Bringing with her all of the conflict and the agonised pleasure that being in the same room with her always engendered.

'Hi. Sorry I've not been around. Anya introduced me to one of the other counsellors. They were both really helpful.'

'Don't apologise. This is what you're here for. I'm not expecting you to follow me around all the time.'

She nodded, hovering between the door and the visitors' chairs, clearly making her mind up which she was going to choose. 'I...um... Anya mentioned something that I'd like to ask you about. At some point...'

'Now's as good a time as any.' Gil waved her to a chair. 'Sit down.'

Clemmie sat, taking her time in hanging her handbag over the back of her chair, and then stowing the notepad she was carrying into it. Obviously this conversation didn't require pen and paper, but it did seem to be taking its time to get started. Gil waited.

'Anya said that you've suffered from retrograde amnesia.'

A knot tightened suddenly in his stomach. He'd decided to follow Clemmie's lead, and that was what he'd do.

'Yes, that's right.'

'It's something I'm interested in. I was wondering if I could know a little more about what happened to you.' The tips of her ears were glowing red now. This meant something to Clemmie, as well.

'Of course.' Gil leaned back in his seat, trying to collect his thoughts. He should just start at the beginning and find out where that went. That went a little against the grain; he liked to be prepared in these kinds of situations.

'I was injured playing rugby. I don't remember what happened, but I'm told I collided with one of the other players, and then got up again and continued playing. I left the club after the match and four hours later Sam Gordon found me sitting in A & E, here at Barney's. I hadn't checked in and no one knew I was there, until Sam found me.'

'You were just sitting there?' Clemmie gave him a horrified look and Gil felt himself flush with embarrassment.

'Admitting I needed help wasn't my strong point and I was probably on autopilot by then. I imagine I was looking pretty grim by that stage, and since Sam's a neurosurgeon, she was well aware of the symptoms. It was my good luck that she happened to be there at all—she had been called down to see a patient. I'm told I didn't express much gratitude at the time, and objected very vociferously when she tried to examine me.'

'She probably saved your life.' Clemmie was staring at him now, and it was Gil's turn to look away. He knew how close he'd come...

'She did. Sam used to say that I was her first diagnosis in the wild, and she assisted in my surgery. After that she took a particular interest in my case and that's how we first became friends.'

'And you don't remember any of that.' Clemmie seemed to be homing in on what he did and didn't remember.

'The first thing I remember is waking up in the neurosurgical unit, two weeks later. I was very disorientated, and hardly even knew who I was. I regained most of my memories pretty quickly, but there's a complete blank starting two weeks before my injury and running through to two weeks after it.'

'And you have no memory at all of what you were doing for any of that time?'

'Nothing. I've been told about the circumstances of my injury and what happened after that, but no one can tell me about the two weeks before.' Gil carefully omitted a few salient details.

'Why not?'

'I was at a conference, in Manchester. Away from home, and none of my friends could tell me anything about that.'

'Do you have any theories? About why you might have forgotten just that two weeks?' Clemmie looked up at him quickly and then back down at her hands. But that one glance spoke volumes. This meant something to Clemmie and there was a reason behind her questions.

'Stress is often thought to be a contributing factor to retrograde amnesia. I had a high-stress job and my way of dealing with that was not giving myself the time to think about it too much. That's not a healthy way of living.'

Clemmie was nodding slowly, weighing every word he said. And she was giving nothing back. Gil couldn't keep this up, and it didn't bode well for their working relationship either. Knowing that she must remember him, but was deliberately not saying so, wasn't any kind of basis for the trust that was needed when dealing with patients.

Gil waited for her to reply. Then he took his wallet from his desk drawer.

'As I said, I don't remember much about the

conference I went to. But I found this photograph in my wallet, about a month later.'

He laid the snapshot on his desk and Clemmie leaned forward, examining it. He'd waited seven years to find out what this photograph meant, but these moments seemed far more agonising than all the rest. When she finally looked up at him again, Clemmie's eyes were glistening, as if she'd just blinked away tears.

'I thought I recognised you. I wasn't sure.'

'I'm a little different now.' Not *that* different. 'If there's something I have to apologise for, Clemmie...'

She shook her head quickly. 'No. Nothing.'

'I wasn't sure whether I should say anything about it or not. I don't remember anything about that week, and...' He shrugged. 'You might have thought I was a real pain in the neck.'

Clemmie's eyes softened suddenly. 'No. No, I didn't think that. We were friends.'

It was quite a leap from thinking she recognised him, to their having been friends. Gil decided not to mention it.

'That sounds nice.' The regret at what had been lost felt as fresh and new as if it had all happened last week. 'I'm sorry that we didn't stay in touch.'

He would have left it at that, but then Clemmie gave herself away. She reached for the photograph, flipping it over as she did so and glancing at the back before she put it back down on the desk again, face up. She knew what was written on the back…

'I called you.' She pressed her lips together as if even that small detail was too much. 'I know now why I didn't get an answer.'

Then it hit him. Meeting someone, making friends or maybe something more. Then ignoring their calls. She must have thought that he'd ghosted her.

And…when Gil thought about it, that was exactly what he'd done. It had been weeks before he'd asked one of the nurses to help him retrieve his phone from the locker by his bed and charge it, and Gil had clumsily deleted the missed calls and messages, barely looking at them. Those who knew of his injury wouldn't be expecting a reply, and those who didn't… He couldn't bring himself to explain that the man who was calling them back wasn't the one they were expecting to hear from.

Two more *if onlys* to add to the list. If only he'd realised that there would be a time when he could recognise himself again. If only he'd kept those call records and compared them with the number on the back of the photograph. He might have called Clemmie sooner and been able to speak with her.

'I'm so sorry, Clemmie.' It was all Gil could think of to say.

'What for?'

For the way she was kneading her hands together in her lap, the knuckles showing white with tension. For the pinched look on her face. For everything and anything that he might have done, which he couldn't remember.

'I don't know.'

'You've nothing to apologise for, Gil.'

Gil wasn't too sure of that. But whatever the rights and wrongs of it, Clemmie seemed determined not to share, her lips pressed together tightly. Since fate seemed pitted against them, maybe letting the conversation run its course had been a bad idea.

'I should let you go. You must have a train to catch.'

She glanced at her watch, and then nodded. 'Yes, I'll catch the five-forty if I hurry. Perhaps we could talk a bit more another time.'

She was trying to pretend that nothing was wrong. Gil could identify with that—he was making the very same effort. Maybe it was best to leave things here and see how they both felt in the morning.

'Go and catch your train. Have a good evening.'

'Thanks. You too.' Clemmie was suddenly a

blur of activity, jumping to her feet and almost running out of his office.

Gil stared after her, wiping his hands across his face. It had been a long time since the world was this out of control, jumbled thoughts dancing in his head like strangers at a party that he'd wandered into by mistake.

He'd cleared the air between him and Clemmie—or at least he hoped he had. Time would tell. But it still nagged at him that he was sure there was something she wasn't telling him. Something that had hurt her, and which she hadn't been able to brush aside and forget.

Something that she remembered, and he didn't.

CHAPTER SIX

IT WOULD GET EASIER. Clemmie told herself that each morning when she dragged herself out of bed, and each evening when she got home, flung her bag down in the hallway and filled the bath, in the hope that steaming, perfumed water would wash away the ache she felt.

And it did get easier. Making sure that her personal issues didn't get in the way of her work meant avoiding Gil as much as she could. That wasn't difficult. He'd drawn up a list of people that she should spend time with during the first week of her stay here. Physiotherapists, counsellors, the head of the nursing team, and the administrators. The two hours that she spent with Maggie learning how she juggled calls, sign-in sheets and people who had every kind of question were a revelation. She even spent a couple of hours in the early morning with one of the cleaners, listening to an interminable stream of chatter about the little quirks of her job. Clemmie had *thought* that she knew exactly how all the different cogs in the hospital day fitted together, but she was finding out that she really didn't.

She had time to sit down and speak with the patients here too, and was learning just as much from them as she was the staff. Jeannie's bravery, in setting aside her fear of falling again. Jahira's bubbly nature, which was breaking through her difficulties in communicating. Everyone was special and had something to contribute.

At first it was a relief that her communication with Gil had dwindled to a succession of notes, left with Maggie, who voiced her exasperation with the situation and asked Clemmie a couple of times if she couldn't contrive to actually *speak* to him. But even passing him in a corridor made her heart jump, flooding her head with memories of his touch. Watching him approach her was a pure and delicious experience, where every line of his body seemed traced with joy. And then seeing him walk away allowed the resentment back in. How could he have forgotten that he'd fallen in love, when that was supposed to be an experience that changed every fibre of your body?

And then it happened. Clemmie was standing at the reception desk, talking to Maggie, when Gil came hurrying through. He shot his usual brief smile in Clemmie's direction and kept going, despite the fact that Maggie had reached for his messages and was waving them at him.

'Sorry, Maggie. On my way to see Jahira…'

Maggie nodded, stowing the messages back on her desk. Before she could weigh up the advisability of it all, Clemmie followed. If Jahira was having problems, then she wanted to be there for her.

'What's happening, Gil?'

'It's Jahira. Something's upset her.' He didn't slow his pace. 'Shouldn't you be going home?'

'No, I'm supposed to be watching and learning. Even helping out if that's not too much of an imposition.'

He flashed her a querying look. She could have left out that last part; the fact that she hadn't exchanged more than two words at a time with Gil over the last few days was just as much her responsibility as his.

'Of course not. I'm sure I remember giving you access to everything we do here.'

'You did.'

They were agreed on that, at least. Maybe it was time to back off a bit now and show him that she knew how to work as part of a team. As they neared Jahira's room, Clemmie could hear the sound of raised voices, and Gil's pace slowed. It wouldn't help for them to rush in there as if they were the cavalry.

Jahira was sitting in the chair beside her bed, tears rolling down her face. One of the nurses was trying to calm her, but the girl seemed inconsolable. She raised her arm, banging it down hard onto the wheeled over-bed table.

Gil moved swiftly, catching up a pillow from the bed and plumping it down onto the table before Jahira could bang her arm down a second time. Then he backed off, giving the girl some room.

'If you want to let off a bit of steam, you can bang a lot harder than that without hurting yourself.'

Jahira glared at him at first, but then seemed to calm a little in response to the relaxed tone of Gil's voice.

'It doesn't even hurt all that much.'

He nodded. 'Just when you're not banging it, yeah?'

'Yes. That's when I get the shooting pains and the pins and needles.'

Gil nodded. 'That's pretty much the way of it. I can explain exactly why that's happening if you're interested.'

Jahira shook her head. 'Not really.'

The atmosphere in the room was calmer now.

The nurse had melted away, and Clemmie had taken one of the visitors' chairs from the stack in the corner and sat down, assuming that Gil wanted her to keep out of the way but determined that she wanted to be here for Jahira. Gil reached for the second chair.

'So what's going on, then?'

'Everything's...different. *I'm* different.'

'Different how?'

Silence. Gil tried again.

'You know, it's pretty easy to feel that you're different when you can't rely on your arms and legs to do the same things they used to. I'm not sure that makes you a different person, though.'

'You don't understand...' A tear rolled down Jahira's cheek.

'Try me. You're right—I don't understand everything, but I'll listen.'

'Sarah came this afternoon. You know she's my girlfriend?'

Gil nodded. 'Yeah, your mum told me. Were you pleased to see her?'

'I hated it when she came to the hospital. I didn't want her to see me like this but... Here it's not so bad.'

'It's good that you're spending so much of your free time together. Sarah's always welcome here, and she can bring a drink or some sandwiches with her from the café. Call in to my office for an apple.'

Apples again. Clemmie was tempted to roll her eyes, but it made Jahira smile. 'How many apples have you got?'

'Far too many at this time of the year. I'm always on the lookout for someone to help me with them.'

Jahira heaved a sigh. 'Well, I don't know if Sarah's even coming back. We had a hug and a kiss and…she said I was different. Not like I was before…'

'We've talked about feeling different.' Gil floated the idea.

'Yes, but… I didn't think *that* would be different. Was it different for you?'

Gil turned his mouth down in what looked like regret. 'I wasn't in a relationship when I had my brain injury.'

Clemmie had been. With him. It had taken a long time for her to accept that Gil had gone. But then, the complications of that situation weren't really what Jahira needed to hear right now, and he was understandably cautious about giving a seventeen-year-old girl relationship counselling.

'Gil might not be the person you need to ask.' She heard her own voice, and Gil swung round suddenly towards her. From the look on his face, he was grateful for the intervention, and Clemmie reminded herself that she was doing this for Jahira, not him.

'S'pose not.' Jahira shrugged. 'You're going to tell me to talk to Sarah, aren't you?'

'Talking about how you feel is always a good idea, if you feel you can do it. Sometimes it's difficult.'

'I don't even know what to say to her. I love her, and...' Jahira's eyes filled with tears. 'She asked me if I still fancied her. Suppose I don't...'

'I don't think...' Gil lapsed into silence again, probably realising that whatever he did or didn't think wasn't going to help.

'Let's talk about this a bit, shall we?' Clemmie wished she hadn't sat back here now, because Gil's large frame was partly obscuring her view of Jahira. 'Why don't I get us something to drink?'

Gil was on his feet before she could move. 'I'll get the drinks and leave you two to talk.' He waved his hand in an indication that Clemmie should come and sit where he'd been sitting.

'Thanks.' Clemmie gave him a smile that wasn't totally for Jahira's benefit. Leaving now was an expression of trust that she hadn't done a great deal to earn.

'I'll bring some biscuits, as well...'

Jahira grinned at him. 'Those chocolate ones are nice. No apples.'

'Right you are. No apples.'

The last few days had been like walking on eggshells. Gil had recognised the need to give Clemmie some space, and maybe take a little space himself, but he'd yearned for her. Every note, every time he'd caught sight of her, had been precious.

All the same, he was aware that he'd given her a little too much rope, and that their own personal needs were beginning to interfere with his professional goals of giving Clemmie a full understanding of how the unit worked. He'd noticed that she'd missed the staff meeting yesterday, and that was an integral part of communication within the unit. She really should have come to that.

He waited outside Jahira's room for almost an hour, managing to pretend that he was doing something for part of the time, but largely just waiting. It reminded him of when he'd been a patient here, and much of his time had been spent waiting. It had been the polar opposite of being an A & E doctor, where his main aim in life had been to get around to everyone as soon as humanly possible.

He could hear laughter coming from behind the closed door and guessed that what his mother and sisters termed as 'girl talk' was going on. Whatever. If it worked, it worked.

And apparently it had. When she left the room, Clemmie had a broad smile on her face, which slipped a little when she saw Gil.

'Jahira's okay?' That was what Gil really needed to know.

'Yes. It's hard enough working out who you are when you're seventeen, without having a brain injury to deal with. We talked it all over and I've convinced Jahira that her circumstances might have changed but she's still the same person she always was with all the same wants and needs.'

And the same desires. He felt that his desire for Clemmie must have been born seven years ago, and had only lain dormant, waiting for the moment he laid eyes on her again. Such was the force with which it had burst back into his life.

'And Sarah?'

Clemmie shrugged. 'From what Jahira says, it sounds as if Sarah wants things to be back the way they were, and she's just going through a few difficulties over knowing exactly what to say. We talked about some ways that Jahira might ask for what she needs, and I said that I'd talk to them both the next time Sarah visits.'

That all sounded good. Clemmie was looking at him expectantly, and he should say something.

'Thank you. I'm glad you could spare the time to come and talk to her.'

Clemmie nodded. 'Always. She's a good kid.'

And Clemmie was a good woman. He tried his best to be a good man, and this couldn't go on. Clemmie's advice to Jahira had been spot on.

'I think *we* need to talk, too.'

'That would be good. Your office?'

'It can wait. Don't you have a train to catch or something?'

'There's always another one.'

She turned on her heel and started to make for his office. Gil followed her, retreating behind his desk and waving her into one of the visitors' chairs. He supposed that this was a work conversation, even if he had a strong suspicion that whatever was bugging Clemmie had very little to do with their work.

'I…um…have the impression that you've got a few issues about working with me. If it's because of our conversation the other day…'

Her eyes darkened. There was something there, in his forgotten past, and he wished that Clemmie would just say it.

'If I've done something wrong, I need you to tell me about it because I don't remember.'

She shook her head. 'There's nothing. We were acquaintances.'

Now he was sure. First it had been a half-forgotten encounter. Then a friendship. Now it was back to an acquaintance, and every nerve in his body told Gil that it was more. If his conscious mind couldn't remember, then maybe his instincts did.

'There's something, Clemmie. I feel it. We're allowing our personal feelings to get in the way of our jobs, and that's unacceptable. I'm to blame, but you're not helping—you didn't even come to the staff meeting yesterday.'

'I was...' Clemmie reddened, shaking her head. 'It doesn't really matter what I was doing. You're right—I know the staff meeting's important and I should have come.'

'It's okay. I'll forward the meeting notes to you.' Gil gave a little in return.

'Thanks.' Clemmie heaved a sigh. 'That's not really the issue, is it?'

Gil shook his head. 'No, not really.'

The room suddenly seemed very quiet. None of the bustle of a busy hospital. He fancied he could hear the sound of birdsong, floating through the open doors in from the garden. This was nice. Even Clemmie's silences seemed to feed his soul.

'All right. We met at the conference and we

talked a lot. We became friends and…there was a connection there. You seemed to get what I was saying.'

Gil felt a lump form in his throat. He got what she was saying now; it all seemed to make sense to him. 'A meeting of minds?'

'Yeah. I'd really hoped that we could continue our friendship, and when you didn't answer any of my calls or messages, it felt as if you'd brushed me away. I thought I deserved a bit more than that and I was very angry with you.'

He'd come to terms with not remembering, but suddenly it felt like a terrible loss. Gil chose his words carefully. 'You did deserve more.'

'I know now why you didn't pick up the phone, and I'm sorry that I was angry with you.'

'It's okay. You came to the obvious conclusion. Did I say that I'd call you?' Since Clemmie was in the mood for honesty, then Gil could risk a little of his own.

'Yes, you did. Obviously you couldn't…' She blushed a little. Clemmie *had* been angry with him.

He took a deep breath. This was so hard to finally say. 'I deleted all of the missed calls from my phone without looking at them. I had your number on the back of the photograph, but

I didn't know who you were and it took me a long time to pluck up the courage to call you.'

'Why?'

Gil wanted to shrug and tell her that he didn't know, but the warmth in her eyes stopped him. This might be the only chance he ever had to tell her how he'd felt, and it seemed to be important to Clemmie.

'I wanted to call. But I had nothing to offer you, or anyone else who had contacted me. I wasn't the same man as the one in the picture.'

'You felt the way that Jahira does now?' Clemmie gave him a look of gentle reproach.

'Yeah. Quite a bit like that, actually. I wondered sometimes if I'd ever be able to get back to what I was before the brain bleed. Reckoned I was just the guy with slurred speech and a useless hand, who fell over quite a lot and forgot everyone's name.' Gil shrugged. 'I had my share of self-pitying moments.'

'It's human.' Clemmie shot him a reproving look. 'And I would have understood.'

'I know you would. I'm the one who didn't understand, and I'm sorry.'

'Apology accepted. I'm sorry that I was angry with you, and that I allowed that to cloud my thinking...' Clemmie fell silent as Gil frowned at her.

'Apology *not* accepted. My mother wasn't

much of a one for advice, but the one thing she told my sisters was that if you call someone three times and they don't get back to you then you give up on them.' The advice had been if they called a *guy* three times, but Gil wasn't comfortable suggesting that he and Clemmie had been anything more than friends. Even if her admission of anger told him one thing very plainly. That she'd been hurt.

But Clemmie seemed to know what he meant. 'That's good advice. Something everyone should know. Can I say that I regret what happened, then?'

Gil nodded. 'That's fair enough. So do I.'

He already felt that maybe he'd said too much, but it was unexpectedly good to talk. A great weight seemed to be lifting from his shoulders, and maybe one last admission on his part would take away some of Clemmie's hurt anger.

'I… I did try to call you. Much later. Your number was unobtainable.'

She stared at him, the tips of her ears going a deep red. 'When?'

'I don't remember exactly…' Gil thought hard. 'It must have been in the new year. I'd made a resolution.'

She shook her head suddenly. 'I had a new phone for Christmas. My number changed…'

Her cheeks were red now, and she was biting her lip.

'Nice present.'

Clemmie shook her head. 'Not so much… My old one turned out to be better.'

The implication that she would have kept her old phone had she known he would call warmed Gil. That Clemmie would have been there for him, despite his having hurt her and taken nearly six months to pluck up the courage to call. It seemed inconceivable that he could ever have been just friends with Clemmie, but Gil had nothing concrete that he could rely on to suggest otherwise. Just a feeling, which could have been the result of staring at Clemmie's photograph for the last seven years, and a lot of wishful thinking.

'Are we good?' Clemmie's voice broke into his thoughts.

'Yes. We're good.' Gil hoped they were. Maybe saying it would make it so.

Clemmie nodded, getting up out of her seat. 'I really should be getting my train.'

'Yeah. Have a good evening.'

He watched her go, and then sank his head into his hands. There had been so much new information in the last couple of days, and he imagined that Clemmie was finding it all as difficult to process as he was. And there was still the nagging feeling that he didn't know everything yet. Maybe he never would. Gil wondered whether the protocol regarding not kissing and telling applied to the person you'd kissed. There probably weren't many precedents for that particular situation.

Would they ever really get past this? They'd talked before, and then retreated into silent avoidance. Maybe this was just too much for either of them to ever really be friends, and the best he could hope for would be Clemmie not seeing him as the enemy.

A knock sounded on the door and he jumped. Clemmie was standing in the doorway, holding a peach.

'I didn't eat this at lunchtime. Swap you for an apple?'

Suddenly the world felt a happier place. Clemmie's bright smile was all he needed to revive his belief that nothing was impossible. He grinned at her.

'Thanks. Don't tell anyone, but I'm in danger of getting a little sick of apples.'

CHAPTER SEVEN

THAT DAMNED PHONE! Harry had given it to her for Christmas, a top-of-the-line new smart-phone. Clemmie had been touched by the gesture; he'd known that she was thinking of getting a phone that did a little more than just make calls, and this was a really nice one. He'd said that the line rental was paid up for two years...

Clemmie shivered at the thought. She'd used that phone a lot, talked to her friends on it and texted them. When the two years were up, she'd wanted to keep it and decided to renew the contract. Harry had been away for the weekend with his friends, and Clemmie had known he didn't like to be interrupted, so she'd gone onto the website and got a new password for the account sent through to her by text.

Then she'd realised. There were numbers that had been blocked. Texts sent. The friends who'd seemed to melt away after she'd got engaged to Harry had been calling her and she'd never known. And Harry would have been able to see who she'd called and when.

That phone had been her worst enemy and now it was her best friend, because it showed her the truth about Harry. Clemmie had searched the house and found a list of all her internet usernames and passwords hidden at the back of his wardrobe. The subtle control he'd exercised over her became suddenly clear. The way he trivialised how she felt and made her doubt her own judgement and memories. The way being around him when he was in one of his moods was like walking on eggshells. These weren't just the symptoms of a marriage that could have been better if she'd tried a little harder. They were all part of a deliberate and systematic violation.

Clemmie had spent the whole afternoon changing her passwords. Then she'd packed her bags and left the following morning, stopping off at Tower Bridge. Wheeling her suitcases to the centre of the bridge and waiting until the water beneath her was clear of boats had felt like a private and overdue ceremony. She'd taken the phone out of her pocket, holding it over the parapet, and as she'd dropped it, she'd said goodbye to Harry for good.

And now Gil had told her that he'd tried

to get in touch with her. His call could have changed everything, her past and her future. Maybe it still could.

Clemmie wasn't sure what to expect when she arrived at work the following morning. She'd spent much of the night awake, and when she'd slept she'd dreamed of Gil. Yesterday had left her feeling that there might be a way forward with him, despite all her fears and doubts, but that might change.

But Gil had clearly abandoned any uncertainties he had, in favour of action. When she reported to his office, she found him sorting sheets of paper into piles and stapling them together.

'It's Budget Review time.' He didn't bother with anything as mundane as a *good morning*.

'I can see you're busy. Do you want me to leave you to it?' Perhaps this was Gil's way of making sure that they didn't have an opportunity to spend too much time together.

'No, I'm hoping you'll help.' He collected the stapled bundles together in a pile and dumped them on the far side of his desk, opposite the visitor's chair.

'But I've no experience of doing budgets.'

'Exactly. It's why you'll need to learn. You

may want to get yourself some coffee before you get settled.'

Clemmie surveyed the pile of papers. 'Yes, I think I will. You want some?' He'd obviously been here for a while and the mug on his desk was empty.

'Thanks, that would be great.' Gil went back to his sorting and stapling, and Clemmie picked up his cup and made for the coffee station.

She'd always imagined that budgets were deadly dull. But she had to admit that Gil's smile, and his dark eyes, added a heady arithmetic to the mix. And *his* budgets were all about what might be done if you thought outside the box, rather than what couldn't be done. The staffing and equipment costs were pretty standard, but exigencies were a world of their own, touched by Gil's ingenious charm.

'You do all this.' She scanned the list of activities. 'On *this*?' The figure at the bottom seemed very small.

'That's the essence of good budgeting. Making it stretch. So, for instance, the figure for the library…'

Clemmie ran her finger down the list. 'Yep. Got it.'

'That figure's for bookshelves only.'

'Okay. So where did all the books come from?'

'There's a bin where patients can put books that they've already read and don't want to keep, and a lot of visitors can be persuaded to bring in whatever they have spare at home. There's an advantage in being a relatively long-stay unit, because we get to know patients and their families, and they're often very willing to help out.'

His grin made Clemmie feel she was about to melt. Pure sex on wheels. It did make rows of numbers seem far more enticing. Maybe she could just sit back and enjoy it. She'd made her decision—work came first—and she wasn't going to go back on that.

'All right. So if we're talking about squeezing as much as we can from as little as possible...' She could have phrased that better, but Gil didn't seem to mind. 'How do you manage the gardening therapy on so little? I would have imagined the garden would be very costly to maintain.'

'We rely on a little help from the landscaping crew here at the hospital, but we also have a team of volunteers who come in to help once a month. They do the bulk of the work. The greenhouses were free, although we had to spend a bit of money on the flooring and other safety elements.'

'Where did you get free greenhouses? They look pretty smart.'

'They were display models that were given to us by a local garden centre. We dismantled them and brought them here and put a notice up saying who'd donated them, and everyone was happy.'

'And someone just knocked on your door and offered you a greenhouse?' Clemmie imagined there had been a bit more to it than that.

'Um…no. I spent a couple of days driving around until I managed to find someone who was willing to help us.'

Clemmie allowed herself a smile. Two whole days, before Gil found someone who would succumb to his charm by giving him a green-house. These garden centre proprietors must have hearts of steel. Gil's obvious enthusiasm for stretching a tiny budget far further than she could have imagined had already made her pulse beat a little faster.

'So what do you think? If you'd like, we could do these together and it would give you an insight into what's required. Or if you'd pre-fer, you could work with Kami in the physio-therapy suite, while I work on the budgets.'

Clemmie had already chatted with Kami, the head physiotherapist in the unit, and although she wanted to spend some more time seeing how she put theory into practice, Clemmie could do that later. Gil had given her a means of escape, but she didn't want to take it.

'I'd like to get a feel for how the budgets work, if you don't mind. It'll stand me in good stead for the future. I can come in a bit earlier tomorrow to give us more time together.'

'Good.' Gil seemed pleased with the outcome of his morning's work so far. 'Then I suppose the best place to start is to take a look through these together.' He turned his computer screen to face her and walked around his desk to sit down next to her. When Clemmie leaned in to see the screen, she caught a hint of Gil's scent. Soap and sex really did go well together.

'Right, then. What am I looking at?'

Gil liked to think that when he applied himself to a problem, he could generally find a way to work through it. That was Clemmie's approach too, she was always looking for ways to say yes instead of reasons to say no, and that made for a great team. Working through things together was more pleasurable than he could have imagined, but maybe he shouldn't be so surprised. Clemmie had said that they'd understood each other when they first met, and that hadn't changed. Why would it? Chemistry was chemistry, and the whole idea of it was that you put two of the same elements together, and they always reacted in the same way.

Clemmie was going to have the best of him from now on. He would give her every insight into the running of the rehab centre that he could, every last piece of experience that might help her to advance her own career. He owed her that, after the way he'd let her down.

And it was working. Clemmie had taken him up on the challenge with such enthusiasm that he was in real danger of being outdone. He wasn't sure if she'd forgiven, and he doubted that she'd forgotten, but her smile told him that she was making as much of an effort as he was to come to terms with the way he'd hurt her and move on.

Two days later, she bounced into his office, looking as fresh as a daisy, even though she must have got up very early to get here at this time. The sombre suits that she'd worn to work until now appeared to be a thing of the past. Yesterday she'd worn a bright top, and this morning Clemmie was wearing a dress, her hair swept to one side and rippling over her left shoulder. The asymmetry really suited her.

'I added up all of these numbers in three ways last night, and they still don't balance.'

Clemmie laid the printed spreadsheet down on his desk and Gil tore his gaze from the soft folds of the fabric that covered the tops of her arms, focussing on the pencil ticks beside each total.

'Good morning.'

She gave him a smile. 'That too.'

He loved the way that just a few words between them were enough to set the day running on its intended course. A few words and a smile.

'You haven't added in the contingency.'

'Ah! Yes, of course. I forgot that the last time, as well. Always expect the unexpected, eh?'

That was one of Clemmie's wry jokes, and it was heartening to find that she finally found some humour in their situation.

'Sometimes the unexpected isn't so bad.'

She reached for an apple from the bag on his desk and sank her teeth into it. Those little signs of friendship were coming to mean so much to Gil. Because Clemmie meant so much to him. She was the reality behind the photograph, a living, breathing woman who was unpredictable and fascinating. Each day she asked more of him, expecting him to forgive himself for the way they'd parted, and put aside his doubts. It was challenging, but her smile gave him the strength to achieve the impossible.

They worked for two hours, and then Clemmie threw her pencil down onto his desk. 'Everything adds up now. Shall we stop here?'

'Yeah, it's time for my morning rounds. Do you have to meet with anyone this morning, or are you coming with me?'

'I'll tag along with you if that's okay.'

Gil nodded, gathering together the papers they'd been working on, and closing down his computer. 'We've made some good headway. I don't suppose you'd like to pop back and help me with the accounts next year, would you?'

She laughed. 'Maybe. But only if you bribe me with apples.'

That was definitely a deal. 'I'll be pruning for an extra-large crop next year. And throw in some strawberries for good measure.'

Clemmie laughed. 'You know I can't say no to strawberries.'

He actually didn't know anything of the sort. Suddenly it didn't matter all that much. If Clemmie was comfortable enough to access the memories that he couldn't, without even realising she was doing it, then that had to be a good portent.

He rose from his seat, stretching the knots from his shoulders. 'Let's go and do the rounds, shall we?'

* * *

Gil's rounds of the patients in the unit generally consisted of checking on the results of any tests that had been done, reading through therapy reports and medication charts, and, most importantly, going to see people. Clemmie knew that there was a lot to be gained from a five-minute conversation with someone, and Gil was one of those doctors who watched carefully and noticed everything. It was one of the things she'd liked about him, and which she was rediscovering now.

'That's it.' He closed the door of Jeannie's room behind them. 'I'm glad to see that Jeannie's confidence is growing, after her fall. Well done on that.'

'Thanks.' Gil always seemed to notice the things that Clemmie did too, and it was gratifying. She shouldn't get too carried away with that, though; it was just something that Gil did with everyone, however special it made her feel.

'I told Kami that I'd drop in on her physiotherapy session with Dave Newman. He's been experiencing cramps in his leg and Kami's a little concerned.' Gil's list of people he had to see and things he had to do was never-ending, and although he never seemed to rush, he got through an enormous amount in his working day.

His phone rang, no doubt someone else wanting to see him. But instead of his usual promise to be there at such-and-such a time, his face darkened.

'We're needed. Reception.'

Gil turned, hurrying along the corridor, and Clemmie followed him. Maggie was kneeling down beside an elderly man who was sitting in one of the easy chairs, and Clemmie recognised Joe, Jeannie's husband. Joe was here every day to see Jeannie, and everyone knew and liked him.

'I can't rouse him, Gil. And he looks awful...'

'Okay. Thanks, Maggie. Let's take a look at him.' Gil bent down beside Joe and Maggie backed away.

'Oh, dear. I hope he's all right. He said he just wanted to sit down for a few minutes before he went in to see Jeannie.' Maggie shook her head. 'Isn't there anything I can do?'

'The phone...' The phone on the reception desk was ringing insistently, and Gil could do without that distraction. Maggie would probably feel better if she had something to do, as well.

'Oh. Yes, of course.' Maggie hurried away, and Clemmie turned her attention to Joe.

Gil had managed to wake him up, and Clemmie could immediately see what Gil's initial diagnosis was.

'Can you hold your other arm up, Joe?' Joe was holding his left arm above his head, but his right arm lay limp at his side.

'Nah.'

'All right. That's fine, no worries. You can put your arm down now.' Gil's gaze flipped towards Clemmie. Joe was exhibiting the three principal symptoms of a stroke: the right side of his mouth was drooping downwards, he couldn't raise his right arm, and his speech was slurred.

She nodded. 'Should I call for a porter?' Joe clearly needed to be taken over to the main building, where there were facilities to scan and treat him.

'No, it'll be quicker if I wheel him over myself. We need to get someone to keep an eye on Jeannie. She'll be expecting Joe.'

'You stay here. I'll organise that.'

No conflict, no second-guessing. That happened when professionals trusted each other, working together to do what was needed. How ever had she managed to get to that place with Gil after everything that had gone between them?

There wasn't time to think about it, just act on it. Clemmie could heave a sigh of relief later.

Speaking to the head nurse and fetching a wheelchair only took a couple of minutes, but by the time she got back, Joe had a lot more colour in his face. It seemed that he was feeling better, because he was arguing with Gil.

'There's no need. I really should go and see Jeannie. I'm late already and she'll be wondering where I am.'

'We should get you checked out first, Joe.'

'But I'm feeling better now.' Joe seemed about to try to get to his feet.

'I've just spoken to James, the senior nurse. He's with Jeannie and he's going to tell her that you've been delayed.' Clemmie smiled down at Joe. 'She'll be okay, and we can make sure that you are, too.'

Joe shook his head. 'It's just one of my turns… I've had them before and I'm always okay afterwards.'

Concern flashed in Gil's eyes. Clemmie knew exactly what he was thinking. If Joe had been experiencing this before, then it was likely he'd been suffering a series of mini strokes. Gil knew all too well about the consequences of ignoring warnings and keeping going.

'We're going to go now, Joe.' He spoke quietly, but very firmly.

Joe clearly didn't much like the idea, but he nodded. Clemmie and Gil helped him out of his seat and into the wheelchair, and Clemmie wheeled him towards the covered walkway that ran between the rehab unit and the main hospital, while Gil walked ahead of them, phoning through to the A & E department.

They were waved through the reception area, and a doctor came to see Joe immediately. All he really needed to do was to sign a few forms and pick up the phone to get Joe an immediate slot for an MRI scan, because Gil was watching Joe carefully, talking to him and gauging all of his reactions.

They stepped outside the cubicle, while a nurse got Joe into a medical gown, and the A & E doctor came to speak to Gil.

'A porter will be along soon, to take him up for the MRI.' The younger doctor was clearly aware of Gil's senior position at the hospital, and had been deferring to him in everything.

'Good, thank you. I'll stay here with him and explain what's happening. You get on to your next patient.'

'Thanks. We've been busy this morning.' The young man hurried away.

'Would you like me to stay? You can go and talk to Jeannie and let her know what's going on,' Clemmie asked.

Gil nodded. 'Do you mind?'

'Of course not. Jeannie trusts you and it's a lot better if the news comes from you.'

Something kindled in his eyes. That word again. Two weeks ago, it would have been unimaginable that she could use the word *trust* in any sentence that referred to Gil, but now it had slipped from her lips without a second thought. And Gil had heard it, the way he heard everything that she said.

'Thanks.'

He could have said more, but Clemmie knew exactly what he meant, and he wasn't thanking her for staying behind here with Joe. She shot him an embarrassed smile, and then the nurse appeared at the entrance to the cubicle.

'We'd better…go and talk to Joe.'

'Yeah.' His gaze held hers for a moment longer than necessary. The warm feeling that flooded through her felt suspiciously like the way she'd felt before all the mistakes had ruined the precious bond between them. And then he turned, walking back into the cubicle. Clemmie followed, her knees shaking a little from the force of the realisation. She and Gil were rewriting the past and building a new friendship together.

'This is all a lot of fuss over nothing. I feel fine now.' Joe was frowning. 'At my age it takes a bit longer to wake up.'

'Joe, when I first saw you, you were really unwell. You've been showing all of the symptoms of a TIA, which is a transient ischemic attack. Some people call it a mini stroke. It can pass very quickly, and you feel fine afterwards. We do need to check you out, though, and make sure that we prevent it from happening again.'

'Leave me here, then. I'll sort things out…' In Joe's estimation, sorting things out clearly involved persuading everyone that he was fine, so that they'd discharge him. He wouldn't succeed, but it would be good if he devoted his energies to something a bit more constructive.

Something softened in Gil's eyes. Maybe he was feeling the same as Clemmie did, that it would be special to have someone who cared as much about you as Joe did for Jeannie.

'I get it, Joe. We've all seen how well you look after Jeannie, but it's time for you to let us take the weight for a little while. Stand down, will you?'

There was sense in Gil's words, but it was the conviction behind them that made them so convincing. Joe puffed out a sigh.

'I suppose it won't do any harm to get this checked out.'

'No, it won't. Clemmie's going to stay here with you and I want you to tell her how many times this has happened before, and any other symptoms you've been having. I'll go back to the unit and keep a close eye on Jeannie for you.'

'Yes. Thanks.' Joe stretched out his hand, and Gil shook it.

He left, shooting Clemmie a smile, and with a reminder for her to call him as soon as she knew anything, which was probably for Joe's benefit. She turned to Joe, picking up the notes from the end of the bed and sitting down to address the question of just how many of these TIAs he'd already experienced.

Joe was wheeled up to the MRI suite twenty minutes after they'd found him in Reception. A swift and appropriate response that stood a good chance of preventing the catastrophe of a full stroke. Clemmie allowed herself a smile. Maybe friendship with Gil wasn't so hazardous to her work after all.

CHAPTER EIGHT

SOMETHING HAD HAPPENED. Perhaps the same thing that had happened seven years ago. Clemmie seemed to understand it in a way that Gil didn't.

But he trusted her now. The idea of putting his destiny in someone else's hands had never gone down too well with Gil, but if he was going to do it, then Clemmie's hands were the ones he wanted.

Jeannie had shed a few tears over Joe, but Gil had made sure that she knew that he hadn't suffered the same devastating after-effects of a stroke that she had, and that he was going to be all right. Clemmie had stayed with Joe until he was transferred up to a ward for observation, and Gil had wheeled Jeannie across to visit him after lunch.

'What's this?' Joe smiled at her. 'You're visiting me now?'

'You silly sausage.' Jeannie took his hand. 'I should be giving you a piece of my mind.'

It was obvious that she'd be doing no such thing. Gil reached into the pocket at the back of the wheelchair and handed her the bag that contained the purchases that Jeannie had made at the hospital shop on the way over. Jeannie propped it on her lap, withdrawing her gifts one by one and giving them to Joe.

'Grapes. Just the thing. Are you going to peel me one?' Joe teased his wife.

'That's enough of that, Joe. I've got you those gardening magazines you like. They should keep you quiet for a while.' Jeannie passed him the magazines, smiling as Joe picked them up, flipping through them.

Clemmie rose from her seat, glancing at Gil. By wordless agreement, they left Joe and Jeannie alone.

'Nice.' Clemmie was smiling. 'I'm glad you stopped at the shop.'

'Jeannie wasn't going to arrive empty-handed.' The sudden wish to put his arm around Clemmie's shoulders was almost irresistible. Just to turn the closeness of this morning into physical reality.

'I need to get back to the unit to see Sally. She's one of our volunteers—she brings her dogs in once a fortnight. You want to stop by the coffee shop on the way and get a take-away?' He started to walk towards the main lobby of the ward, waving to the senior nurse who had promised to keep an eye on Jeannie and call him when she was ready to come back to the rehab unit.

'Yes. That sounds good.'

They strolled through the atrium together, joining the queue for coffee. Then walked back to the rehab unit, enjoying the sunshine of a bright, warm day.

'Do you miss it? A & E?'

'You think I'd be better off working there, still?' Clemmie must have seen what Gil had felt. The rush of adrenaline that made him feel suddenly that bit more alive.

'You've made the rehab unit into one of the best in the country. It would be crazy to suggest you should be anywhere else.' She paused for a moment, sipping her coffee reflectively. 'But you told me that you loved the buzz of emergency medicine.'

He had. But it was the kind of love that had done him no good at all. 'My brain bleed forced me to reassess a lot of things. I thought that I was thriving on the stress, but in fact, it almost killed me.'

'You think that stress had something to do with your injury?'

'No, probably not. I don't remember what happened, but I know that I always played to win, so I wouldn't be surprised if I made a bold tackle—' Gil raised one eyebrow as Clemmie snorted with laughter.

'A bold tackle, eh? You were known for that kind of thing?'

'Always. Didn't I tell you that before?' Gil ventured the question.

'No. But my impression of you was that you had a lot of...momentum.'

It was nice that they could talk about the first time they'd met. There was so much that Gil wanted to know about and now it wasn't quite so much of a no-go area between them.

'I had a bit too much momentum back then. I didn't even know how to stop...' Gil shrugged. 'I often wonder if the stress wasn't a contributing factor in my memory loss.'

Clemmie raised her eyebrows. 'So you think that something stressful happened at the conference.'

It was interesting that she should jump to that one conclusion, when she must know as well as he did that wasn't always the way stress worked.

'No. I think that the way I was living my life was putting me under constant pressure.' Gil slowed his pace, hoping it would give them more time. The conversation was beginning to get very interesting. 'Did I seem stressed at the conference?'

Clemmie considered the question and then shook her head. 'No, you seemed happy. Quite relaxed at times.'

There was something she wasn't telling him, but Gil let it go. They were her memories and Clemmie seemed to be more comfortable with sharing them one piece at a time.

'Then you must have caught me at one of the better times in my life.'

She seemed pleased with the idea. 'So you were under a lot of stress with your job?'

'I was, but stress was already a way of life for me. I come from a family of overachievers.'

'What does that mean?'

Gil took a sip of his coffee, thinking about the question. 'It means…my parents worked hard and had good, fulfilling jobs. They taught their kids to do the same. When I was growing up I only saw the rewards—we lived in a nice house and my dad had a boat. I wanted to be just like them, someone who could go out and get anything I wanted. But what my parents didn't teach us was how to handle the fallout from that attitude.'

'Did they know?' Clemmie asked the all-important question.

'No, I don't think they did. My uncle died from heart failure when he was only forty-seven, and Mum began drinking too much because she couldn't sleep without it. She got help eventually, but none of it was ever talked about, and I didn't know how to deal with weakness or failure. I couldn't admit to it.'

'They pushed you too hard?'

Gil shook his head. 'Nah. That would be the easy answer, but they really didn't. They just set an example and I followed it without question. When I had my brain injury I simply didn't know how to tell them, because I couldn't admit to feeling that I was somehow less than what I'd been before. I didn't call them for months.'

Maybe he shouldn't have said that, because he hadn't called Clemmie either. He could see the shock on her face, but then she pulled a regretful smile.

'The way you didn't call me? That's almost reassuring. I don't feel quite so singled out now.'

The consequences of his actions began to sink home. 'Don't ever feel that way, Clemmie. It was all me, and nothing to do with you. I can't say how sorry I am—'

She reached up, putting her finger against his lips. It was all Gil could do to stop them from forming the shape of a kiss. 'You've said sorry already. Apology accepted, so we can move on now, eh?'

Gil nodded. 'I won't make those mistakes again.' He meant it. An apology didn't mean much unless it was accompanied by change.

'So was it your decision to move out of emergency medicine?'

Gil smiled. 'If you're wondering whether I changed course for medical reasons, then no. I could have gone back to my old job, but I realised I was there for the wrong reasons. At work they used to call me a Stress Eater, but in truth, I was only internalising the stress. I was proud of the fact that I didn't need to talk about it and couldn't see that the colleagues who did were the ones who were really coping.'

'Everyone needs to talk.' Clemmie pressed her lips together thoughtfully.

'Yeah. It took losing the very basic things, like being able to feed myself and walk across a room, before I realised that.' It had taken Clemmie's arrival to make him realise that he still had a few outstanding issues and that he didn't talk enough, even now. 'Pride's a hard thing to let go of.'

'You're not proud of what you've achieved here? You should be.' She raised her eyebrows.

Gil chuckled. 'Well...yeah. It's different,

though. I handle stress differently, as well. I've learned that I can't work every waking hour and then blow it all off with a game of rugby at the weekend. That kind of machismo doesn't do me any favours, and it doesn't do my patients any favours either.'

Clemmie nodded, smiling suddenly. 'You've found the place that's right for you, then.'

'Yes. I think so.'

They were nearing the path that ran around the back of the rehab unit, and Gil wondered whether Clemmie would turn to go into the building. But she followed him as he walked to the small walled garden to one side of the greenhouses.

This was one of his favourite places. Donated by an elderly lady who had spent time here after a stroke, it had an air of peace and quiet, away from the activity of the hospital. Raised beds on three sides meant that patients could reach to touch the scented flowers and herbs that grew here, and the central paved area was shamrock-shaped, giving three separate areas where groups could sit and talk.

Sally was already here, along with her two dogs. The gentle animals were used to being stroked and petted, and the giant Bernese mountain dog lay sprawled in the sun, while Zaffie, the golden retriever, was sitting with

Jahira and Sarah, enjoying the fuss that both girls were making of her.

'Everything all right, Sally?' Gil addressed the dogs' owner.

'Yes. I dare say a few more people will be coming out soon. I've let the nurses know I'm here.' Sally lowered her voice. 'How's Joe?'

Gil knew that the unit was a close-knit community, but was constantly surprised by how far and how fast news travelled. 'He's doing well. I've taken Jeannie over to see him, so she won't be coming out to sit with you today.'

'Well, give her my love, won't you? Tell her I'm glad that he's okay.'

'Will do. Thanks for being here today, Sally.'

'My pleasure, Gil. Particularly on such a lovely day.'

Gil turned, pleased to see that Clemmie was still with him, despite all of the opportunities she'd had to go and do something else. He hadn't finished his coffee yet, and so he walked over to the bench outside the greenhouse, sitting down there. Warm pleasure enveloped him when Clemmie followed him, sitting down next to him.

'So how about you? What made you go into neurological rehab?' It was the kind of question that she could answer at almost any level she liked, but Gil was hoping that she might tell him a little more about herself.

'My reasons haven't changed.'

'Uh. We've had this conversation before, haven't we?'

'Yes, but that's okay. I don't mind repeating myself.'

Again, he got the feeling that she was reaching back. Maybe testing out each memory before she shared it, to see if they were still tainted by those unreturned phone calls. Gil hoped that Clemmie was finding that they weren't.

'It'll be the last time. I'll make sure I don't forget *this* conversation.' How could he? The warmth of a scented afternoon, with Clemmie sitting by his side.

She smiled. That made the afternoon complete.

'I spent most of my time with my gran when I was little. Working parents…' There was a hint of wistfulness in her tone.

'A lot of people work and still have time for their kids.'

Clemmie chuckled. 'That's new. You didn't say that last time.'

'We're breaking new ground, then. Maybe I've changed a bit more than I think.' That would be down to Clemmie. Having to re-examine himself so that he could connect with her.

'Maybe you have.' She nudged him gently, in a sign that she liked the change. 'You're right. A lot of parents work, but mine were…absorbed. They didn't seem to have much interest in me, and I didn't feel they really saw me.'

'Their loss.' Clemmie's as well, growing up with that kind of neglect.

'Well, my gran made up for all of that. But she developed dementia and had to go into a nursing home when I was thirteen. I used to visit her every day after school, and I got to know most of the residents there.'

'And you got used to speaking with people who have those kinds of challenges?'

'Yes, I did. I learned not to worry when Gran couldn't remember something, or she didn't know who I was. She knew I was someone and that I was there, and that was enough. And when she *did* recognise me it felt like a really good day.'

'Not everyone has the patience to wait for those good days. Particularly teenagers.' It sounded a lonely way to live, particularly for someone so young who didn't seem to have much parental support.

'When they came they were worth it. Gran was always the one who saw me for who I was.'

Clemmie had said something like that before. That they'd clicked, and she'd felt he understood her. Gil was beginning to realise just how important that would have been in her life. And how much she must have been hurt when he'd seemed to abandon her.

Not just then, but now, too. He'd allowed her to go her own way, spending most of her time talking to everyone else in the unit apart from him. Gil had thought that it was what Clemmie wanted and gone along with it, but maybe it was just what she feared the most. She'd hung on to her anger like a shield, and taken herself out of his orbit, before he could reject her again.

He resisted the temptation to apologise again, because he knew Clemmie wouldn't accept it. 'So you decided to specialise in neurological issues.'

'Yes. I wanted to help give people a chance to get back into their lives again. Society tends to turn its back on those who can't communicate the way everyone else does. Or who don't remember. You understand that, don't you?'

'Yes, I do. For a long time I felt that there was a barrier between me and everyone else, and that I was too slow and couldn't remember the right words. The world was going too fast for me, and a lot of people don't stop and wait.'

'Unseen and unheard.' A melancholy smile hovered around her lips. If only Gil could kiss it away…

'You should never be either of those things.'

She smiled suddenly. 'I've learned that sometimes you have to make a little more noise.'

He cupped his hand behind his ear, hoping that the gesture might tell her that he was listening now. And that he'd listen for as long as Clemmie would allow him to, because time with her was becoming more and more precious, with each day that passed.

She got it. Clemmie laughed, a look of sweet knowingness dancing in her eyes. Gil was becoming more and more sure about the time they'd spent together at the conference. That he'd felt the way he felt now. That when they'd talked it had been more than just a pleasant way to pass an evening. It would have been like food and drink to him. And if he'd been the one who was guilty of smashing all of that to pieces, he could be the one to mend it, as well.

Clemmie had said more than she'd meant to. But that didn't seem so bad, because Gil understood, and coming to an understanding with him had become important to her.

They sat in silence as she finished the rest of her coffee. It was almost cold now, but she didn't want these moments to end too soon. Then she saw James, one of the senior nurses, wheeling a patient along the path that led to the walled garden.

'Ah, good. I'm glad that Edward's made it out here. I told him that there would be dogs here this afternoon.'

Gil laughed softly. 'You've been passing the time of day with my patients again, haven't you?'

'No more than you do.'

'That's okay, then. Edward likes dogs?'

'Yes. He's a volunteer dog walker for his local rescue shelter. He was grilling Jahira about her plans to become a vet the other day.'

'Really?'

'Yes. They've struck up quite a friendship. As unlikely as that might seem.'

Gil nodded. 'Brain injury's a great leveller, sometimes. It's good that Edward is making friends. He's finding the after-effects of his stroke very hard to deal with.'

Clemmie nodded. Edward was in his seventies, a widower and career soldier. She knew that it irked him that his back wasn't as straight as it had been, and that he had to be pushed from place to place in a wheelchair, but he bore it with a quiet resignation. When none of the nurses was able to knot Edward's tie in quite the way he liked it, it had been Jahira who had come to the rescue, insisting that Sarah give it a go. It had taken a few attempts and a stream of advice from Jahira before Sarah achieved the desired effect, but Edward had been pleased that his appearance was finally back up to scratch.

They both got to their feet at the same time. Clemmie knew that Gil was seldom too busy to greet a patient, and Edward waved cheerily at their approach.

'How are you feeling today, Edward?' Gil asked.

'Much better, thank you.' That seemed to be Edward's stock answer, irrespective of how he was actually feeling. 'Can't complain at all.'

'You're going to the walled garden?'

'Yes. Jahira tells me that I should come and help with the dogs.'

Clemmie saw Gil suppress a smile. Since she'd sat down with Jahira and Sarah, and talked through how they both felt, their relationship had improved. Jahira was still struggling, but she was beginning to settle in and become a force to be reckoned with. She'd obviously realised that Edward liked to make himself useful and had asked him to come and help.

'I'm going that way. May I walk with you?' Clemmie asked Edward.

'That would be my pleasure.' Edward's blue eyes twinkled with old-fashioned charm.

'I'll leave you both to it, then.' Gil gave her a smile and then turned to James. 'I'd like to review a couple of the medication sheets with you, if you have a moment...'

James nodded, and the two men headed back to the building together. Clemmie pushed the wheelchair into the walled garden, and when the girls caught sight of them, Sarah jumped to her feet, making room for Edward in between her and Jahira. Sensing the possibility of some attention, the Bernese mountain dog got to its feet, ambling over to him, and Edward smiled, holding out his hand to greet the animal.

CHAPTER NINE

CLEMMIE HAD STAYED in the garden, talking to Sally about the dog visiting schemes here and at her own hospital, and comparing notes with her. Gil had been busy all afternoon, but that was okay. She had a list of people to see, and this separation was just the result of needing to be in two different places, rather than being terrified about getting too close to Gil.

She was on her way to his office, to share an idea with Gil, when she saw him out in the garden, digging one of the flower beds. He'd changed into a pair of worn jeans, and Clemmie stopped for a moment at the window to watch him. Many washes had the advantage of softening denim and making it fit very well. When that was combined with physical activity and a great body, what was a girl to do, but stand and stare for a moment?

Just a moment, though. Clemmie walked out into the garden, trying to keep her mind off the

ANNIE CLAYDON

135

great body, because she was going home, and she couldn't take Gil with her.

'You're just off?' He straightened when he saw her, driving the spade into the freshly dug earth.

'Yes. I've an idea I want to run past you first. I see you've found something else to do.'

Gil chuckled. 'This is recreation.'

'You're sure about that? Looks like work to me.' Hard physical work maybe. But Gil was smiling and relaxed.

'What's your idea, then?' Gil's undivided attention always made her feel good. As if her ideas were worth hearing.

'I'd like to make a memory book, for Jahira and Sarah—'

'Jahira *and* Sarah?' He picked up on her point immediately. Memory books and photographs were one way that families were encouraged to help patients in the unit, but they were usually made for just one person.

'Yes, both of them. I was talking to them today and Jahira remembered something that Sarah didn't. They laughed about it, but I could tell that Sarah was a bit puzzled.'

Gil nodded. 'Forgetting things isn't confined to patients with brain injuries. It can be a different process, though.'

'Exactly. The difference between forgetting

where you put your car keys and forgetting you even have a car.' Clemmie used the analogy she'd heard when she was a teenager and the manager of her gran's care home had explained dementia to her. 'That puts a responsibility on the people around a patient with a brain injury. They're a repository for their memories, but all memory is subjective.'

'You mean that Sarah can tell Jahira the facts, but she might leave things out that were important to Jahira, and her feelings about those facts will necessarily be slightly different.' He stopped to think for a moment. 'And you're talking just about Sarah and Jahira, are you…?'

He was far too perceptive. But then, the whole point of what Clemmie was saying was that memory was a two-way process sometimes.

'Not entirely.'

His face softened. 'I don't want to put pressure on you, Clemmie. Whatever you want to tell me about things that happened that I don't remember…' Gil shrugged. 'It's all a bonus.'

There were things that she definitely *didn't* want to tell Gil. Clemmie was feeling guilty about keeping things from him, but it was better he didn't know about their brief love affair. It would put too much strain on their working relationship, and on the friendship that she was beginning to value so much.

'It's not you, Gil. It's the situation that makes me feel pressured. Wanting to explain things to you and knowing that I can't because I was looking at things through my eyes and not yours. You can be a storehouse for facts, but memories are a very different thing. Sarah's struggling with the same thing—she can tell Jahira what happened on any particular day, but she can't tell her how she felt or see it through her eyes.'

Gil brushed his fingers across the back of her hand. The small gesture told Clemmie everything. About how he was struggling now, and how important this all was to him.

'So Jahira's memory book will be all about how she fits in. With Sarah, with her family...'

'Yes. The memories in it are theirs, and Jahira can add her own to them. Maybe it'll help her work things out a bit.'

Gil nodded. 'I think it's a great idea. A nice slant on something we do so often that we don't always think about how it might really work. Is there anything I can do to help?'

Clemmie laughed. 'You're not just talking about Jahira and Sarah, are you?'

His gaze melted into hers. 'No. I have a personal agenda, too.'

That sounded so much like one of Gil's smiling invitations up to his room at the conference hotel. Her memories changed everything, turning Gil's everyday charm into something he probably didn't mean it to be.

'It's been a good talk, Gil. Thank you. I'll suggest the idea to Jahira and see what she and Sarah think about it.'

'I don't need to tell you to go gently. You have a talent for that without my interference.' He turned suddenly, bending to pick up a bottle of water that was propped on the grass and taking a swig. 'If you've got a moment, I have something to show you.'

Always. These days she always had a moment for Gil, even if it meant missing her train. There would always be another train, and Clemmie's fear over holding on to her time with Gil was diminishing.

She followed him over to a patch of earth behind the greenhouses, and Clemmie saw four big plant cloches. Gil opened one of them, parting the leaves carefully to reveal a large red strawberry.

'Our first one. They're coming into fruit a little later than mine at home.' He grinned up at her.

'Wonderful!' Clemmie crouched down next

to Gil to examine the plants. 'You'll have a lot
more soon. There are plenty of little ones there.'

Gil nodded, reaching out and picking the
strawberry. 'Hold out your hand.'

It looked very tempting. 'No… Gil, you
should save it for someone else…'

'Too late. I've picked it now. When the others are ready I'll get everyone out to pick them
and we'll share them out, but you can't do that
with just one.' He gestured towards the building. 'And no one will see.'

They were hidden behind the greenhouses
and this felt like a delicious secret. Clemmie
held out her hand, and Gil dribbled some of the
water from his bottle over the strawberry to
clean it. Clemmie picked it up and took a bite.

'Mmm… That's…so good. Try it.' She offered the remaining half of the strawberry to
him.

'My hands are dirty…' He grinned suddenly.
'And I'm rather enjoying the look on your face.'

'And you're not going to share?' Clemmie
joked. 'Try it.'

She held the strawberry out, and Gil took a
bite. A sudden, potent reminder of feeding each
other strawberries, on a warm day. Only then,
they'd been sprawled across Gil's bed.

'That's good. You finish it.' His gaze was on
her mouth, and Clemmie shivered as she took

the last bite. A memory that they could both keep, which echoed the memories only she had. It couldn't do any harm, out here…

She couldn't tear her gaze from his face, and as Gil slowly rose to his feet, she followed. They were standing close, but even that physical proximity was less potent than the look in his eyes.

'Clemmie…' He murmured her name, and suddenly she had no choice. Clemmie reached up, pulling his head down so she could plant a kiss on his lips.

One wasn't enough. Of course not. What could she have been thinking? Gil's hands circled her waist, not quite touching the fabric of her dress. She didn't care if he got a few smudges of dirt on her—she just wanted to be close to him. For their bodies to touch when they kissed again.

Somehow that happened, even though she wasn't aware of moving towards him. His kiss was just as spectacular as the last time, and still so different from anything she'd experienced. That was because it was Gil doing the kissing, and his gaze that she seemed to be falling into.

But this was wrong. She could be honest with him, to a point, if they were friends. She could keep that hard-won self-determination. But if they went any further, she'd have to admit the things she hadn't said, their relationship and the mistakes she'd made as a result of it. She'd have to be prepared to give herself to him completely, because that was all she knew how to do with Gil.

When she drew back, he let go of her immediately. He gave a nod, but his eyes were full of questions. Then it hit her.

This was his first time. He didn't remember kissing her before, and he didn't know how much she liked it. She reached up, brushing her fingers against his cheek.

'That was a lot better than strawberries.'

He grinned, a look of relief showing in his face. 'Strawberries? I've just forgotten strawberries?'

Clemmie dug her fingers in his ribs and he laughed. 'I'll have to reacquaint you with strawberries, Gil. No one should forget them.'

His gaze searched her face, and then he nodded. He understood. He knew that their history together outweighed anything that they could do now, even if he couldn't remember all the details.

'You're right, Clemmie. It wouldn't be smart to take this any further.'

'However nice it was.'

'Nice doesn't really cover it.' Gil heaved an

exaggerated sigh. 'Don't you have a train to catch?'

Trains. The old excuse had come to their rescue this time, because if she stayed here much longer Clemmie was going to throw caution to the wind and kiss him again.

'Yes, I think I do. Have you finished here?' Maybe he'd walk her out. She still couldn't quite bring herself to leave him.

'No, I've a bit more to do. But I'm missing you already.' Gil knew what they had to do and was pushing her gently in the right direction.

'See you tomorrow, then.' Clemmie was missing him too, and missing everything else that had followed their very first kiss.

As she walked back towards the unit, she heard the sound of his spade cutting into the earth as he started digging again. Maybe this gardening thing wasn't so crazy after all. Clemmie could do with a little activity, to take her mind off the tingles of pleasure that were still coursing through her. Perhaps if she ran all the way to the station, she could catch her train.

Neither of them had mentioned their kiss yesterday, and Gil felt that was the best way to handle it. Let it be one, isolated incident that made no promises and set no precedents. But it had changed them both subtly.

It felt almost as if they were a couple, as they walked out of the rehab unit together at lunchtime, going to the cafeteria to buy coffee and sandwiches and then on to the park, to meet Sam. Gil saw her sitting on a bench, moving the double buggy back and forth, and as they got closer, he could hear the sound of the twins crying.

'Hey. Where's Yanis? You didn't come down here on your own, did you?' Gil put the coffee down on the bench, along with the sandwiches and a bag of apples that he'd brought along with him.

'No. He's popped into Neurosurgery to do a couple of urgent things.' Sam sighed. 'I'm not even allowed in the building.'

'Quite right, too. You're on maternity leave.' Gil grinned. When he'd called Sam to ask about meeting up, Sam had declared that she would be delighted to pop into the rehab unit, and Gil had suggested the park as a compromise.

One of the twins had settled a bit, and the other was still crying. Gil bent, and, when pulling a face didn't work, he picked the tiny baby up, walking around in a circle and jiggling her in his arms. She miraculously stopped crying, and when he looked up, both Sam and Clemmie were staring at him.

'You're a baby whisperer, Gil!' Sam grinned broadly. 'Or is this just your natural charm?'

Clemmie was smiling too, and Gil avoided her gaze, concentrating on the baby in his arms. A kiss was one thing. He hadn't anticipated that being in close proximity to both Clemmie *and* the twins would make his heart melt so very quickly.

But whatever Clemmie was thinking or feeling, she was keeping it to herself. She sat down on the bench, taking two of the cardboard cups from the holder and passing one to Sam. The two women introduced themselves, without any need for Gil to intervene.

'Shall I take them for a walk? Um… Aurelie seems a bit happier now.' Gil felt a trace of reluctance in letting the tiny baby go as he bent to put her back into the buggy.

'Nice try, Gil. That's Charlotte.' Sam grinned. 'If you don't mind, walking always does seem to settle them. Don't be too long, or I might eat your sandwiches. I'm really hungry.'

'Help yourself.' Gil shot Sam and Clemmie a smile and started to push the buggy along the wide path that ran around the edge of the park.

'What do you think, then, ladies?' As he walked, he bent towards Charlotte and Aurelie, checking that they were both all right. 'Will Clemmie be okay on her own?'

Of course she would. Gil had the same confidence in Clemmie that he had in Sam, and when he glanced behind him, the two women were already deep in conversation. Coffee in the park would go perfectly well without his input, and he was much better employed in keeping the twins quiet.

Gil named a few of the trees and shrubs that he could see and threw in a couple of gardening tips for good measure. Charlotte—or was it Aurelie?—began to fret a little and he picked up his pace.

'Hey, none of that. I'd like you to think about something for me.' The little one quietened down and Gil kept talking. 'There's this person I know…'

He knew that the twins couldn't focus on him properly at this distance, but the sound of his voice seemed to be keeping their attention. It was soothing to Gil as well, finally being able to say the things that he hadn't shared with even his closest friends.

'She's beautiful and kind, and good at her job. Great sense of humour—you'll find that's important in a partner when the time comes.' He hoped that Aurelie and Charlotte were taking note. This was all useful information for them.

'We've got a past, though. That's not a good

thing, in case you were wondering. And it's confusing for me because I don't remember it. That's a very long story, so I'll skip that part. My main worry is that I don't want to hurt her. I know I hurt her before, and I don't think she's told me everything, even now.'

Gil felt his eyes mist with tears, and he blinked ferociously. There was something about talking to a baby that set your emotions going. Two were an even more potent mix.

'But I just can't back away from her. I… um…' Aurelie and Charlotte didn't need to know the details of exactly how he felt about Clemmie.

'To be honest with you, I kissed her yesterday. I didn't mean to—it just happened—but it was the best kiss…' Gil fell silent, reliving those moments as he walked.

'I don't want to make the mistakes I made the first time around, though. Even if it means we'll only ever be friends, I think it's better to take what we have and be grateful for it.' He stared down at his two confidantes. 'What do you think?'

Charlotte and Aurelie seemed to agree. At least they didn't voice any objections. Gil smiled down at them both.

'Thanks, ladies. Great chat. I appreciate it.' He could see two pairs of eyes beginning to close and reckoned that he'd given the twins enough to think about for the time being.

'Gil!' He heard Yanis's voice behind him and turned. 'Where's Sam?'

'I left her with Clemmie, back on the bench where we found her.' Gil grinned. 'Sam's looking after the sandwiches, so if we hurry, there might be some left.'

Yanis laughed, peering into the buggy at his daughters. 'Nice job. Now they're asleep, shall we go see if we can rescue some lunch?'

Gil nodded, and the two men turned, walking back towards where Clemmie and Sam were sitting.

'Sam's been very keen to meet Clemmie. She seems nice…' Yanis floated the idea.

Gil didn't take the bait. Sam was one of his dearest friends, and he'd become close to Yanis as well, even though he'd only known him a short time. But he'd got his answer from the twins, who were very good listeners and less challenging to talk to than anyone he'd ever met. Even Anya could take a leaf from their book.

'She's a great doctor. Lots of good ideas. I think this working relationship is going to benefit us both.'

Yanis nodded, raising his arm to wave as he saw Sam catch sight of them. Clemmie looked up from the writing pad she had perched on her knees, and her smile seemed warmer than the sun.

It was nice. A summer's afternoon in the park, and friends to share it with. Even if this wasn't all that Gil wanted from his relationship with Clemmie, he was determined that it would be enough.

CHAPTER TEN

CASUAL. NOT TOO casual because she'd be working. Not too smart because it was Saturday, and she wasn't going to the hospital. Smart/casual. Or casual/smart. After half an hour of looking through her wardrobe, Clemmie wasn't entirely sure what the difference was.

This shouldn't be so difficult. She and Gil were going to be spending an afternoon giving the budget proposals a final look-through, uninterrupted by the many other calls on his time that made it much easier to do it at his house than at work. What she wore wasn't going to make the slightest difference to that. Clemmie reached for the dark red dress that was her current go-to piece for any occasion, and slipped into it before she could change her mind again.

Maybe they'd talk a bit, as well. Since Gil had promised lunch, it would be rude to sit there in silence, and Clemmie was beginning to value the time they'd spent getting to know each other again. And if not, the afternoon wouldn't be a complete washout because the budgets would be finished and ready to send off. Clemmie now understood exactly how they worked, and how to get the very best from the money available, and that was an achievement in itself.

'Go with the flow, Clemmie.'

She murmured the words to herself as she glanced into the mirror. This wasn't the battle of wills that she'd had to endure with her ex-husband, who'd had a habit of deciding what he wanted from each and every transaction and sticking to it come hell or high water. It was perfectly possible to spend an afternoon with Gil without arming herself with a thousand answers to questions he probably wouldn't ask.

She picked up her briefcase and car keys and snagged the bag of macadamia nuts that she'd bought to take with her from the kitchen. Hopefully he still liked them, and if he didn't, then she could always eat them herself. Because this afternoon, she *was* going to go with the flow.

It was just lunch. Simple enough. Someone cooked, you sat down and picked up a knife and fork, and you ate.

But Gil saw every day how the simplest things in life could suddenly become mountains to climb. How many times had he patiently picked up a dropped knife or fork and encouraged someone to try again?

'Not the same thing, Gil.' He moved his finger quickly before it suffered the same fate as the cucumber he was slicing. 'There's no reason you can't do this, so just get on with it.'

The doorbell put him out of his misery, by prompting a wash of excitement. The same feeling that engulfed him every time he saw Clemmie, and which came to his rescue and propelled him into action.

How did she do that? It was the same question that occurred to him every time, as well. Clemmie was standing on the doorstep looking like the combination of the girl next door, who he'd known all his life, and an intoxicating new paramour. Effortlessly beautiful. Although he imagined that probably *some* effort had gone into her appearance—her hair shone as if it had been brushed a hundred times, and her eyes looked even more luminous with the application of a little make-up.

'Are you going to let me in?' She grinned at him. 'If not, perhaps you'll bring a chair out and I can wait here in comfort.'

Gil stepped back from the door, still speechless with admiration. Clemmie either didn't notice or maybe she just liked the effect that she had on him. He very much liked it too, so that was one thing they could agree on.

She was a charming guest. Pushing a bag into his hands and looking around her with obvious curiosity. Clemmie peered through the open door of the sitting room, and then gave him a little smile, as if she took pleasure in finding out what all the rooms in his house looked like. When he showed her through to the kitchen, she saw the bowls that were standing ready on the counter.

'Hm. Peanut sauce and a chicken marinade. That's not so difficult to guess. We're having chicken satay?'

'Yep. It's the Malaysian version.'

'Of course. You learned to make it in Malaysia?'

He must have mentioned that he'd been to Malaysia, but Gil didn't remember. Clemmie did, though, and that didn't seem quite as much of a challenge as it had once been.

'No, I wasn't much interested in cooking when I went. I got the recipe from a book, but it tastes much the same.'

'I can't wait, then.' She smiled again, and this time Gil remembered to return the gesture. 'If it tastes as good as this marinade smells, I'll have to get the recipe from you.'

'You can help if you like.' Gil unhooked an

apron that he never used from the back of the door, and she nodded and took it. She had to fold it over at the waist so it would fit her, but she looked enchanting in it.

Clemmie grilled a mean satay, as well. The same recipe tasted a great deal better when she cooked it, or maybe it was just her company that made the difference. Gil pulled the awning down to shade the paved area at the back of the house, and they ate outside. Coffee, macadamia nuts and the first two pears from the tree, which had obligingly ripened this morning, were an easy dessert, and then they set to work.

It took all afternoon to check through the budgets and assemble the package, to be sent off on Monday. Finally they sat grinning at each other, the wrapped parcel sitting on the table between them.

'Done. This is the first year I've had them in early.'

'Thanks, Gil. I've really learned a lot from this.'

'Coffee? Or do you think something to drink is a bit more appropriate to celebrate?' The solar-powered lights that he'd planted amongst the shrubs were beginning to glimmer faintly now, in the early dusk, and Gil gathered up the scrap paper from the table, taking it into the kitchen to put into the recycling bin. When he

turned around, Clemmie was standing right
behind him.

'Do you have the ingredients for that cappuccino cocktail you used to make? Only you need
to go easy on the alcohol. I'll be driving later.'

He'd made her cappuccino cocktails. And
he'd shared his own, very special secret recipe with her. The thought hit Gil like a blow to
the chest, because he knew exactly what that
meant...

The echoes of his own shock registered
in her eyes, and Clemmie's hand flew to her
mouth. 'I've said the wrong thing, haven't I?
I'm sorry...'

'It's okay.' He smiled, trying to make a joke
of it. 'I only used to make cappuccino cocktails
for very special people.'

Clemmie reddened a little. 'Special as in...
good doctors? Valued colleagues?'

She knew that wasn't what he meant. And
finally Gil felt that it wouldn't be so bad to ask,
even if it was in a relatively roundabout way.

'People I like. My brother and I read about
them when we were kids and tried them with
instant coffee and some wine we managed to
sneak out of the kitchen.'

Clemmie winced. 'Ew! That sounds horri-
ble.'

'It made us both sick. We spent a good portion of our teens perfecting the recipe and I managed to get it right for his twenty-first birthday. I don't remember sharing that recipe with anyone else. It was always our thing.'

'I'm honoured, then.' Suddenly her gaze met his. It seemed to draw him in, and before he could stop himself, Gil had taken a step closer.

'Was there anything more than just cappuccino cocktails, Clemmie?'

She thought for a moment. Clemmie must know the answer. She was just wondering whether she'd tell him or not. Then she stepped towards him.

'Yes, there was something else.'

The look in her eyes almost brought him to his knees. Clemmie laid her hand on his shoulder, as if testing him out, and he smiled. Then she stretched up, planting a kiss on the side of his mouth.

'There was this, too.'

Not just that. Fire seemed to be dancing between them, following the path of her fingers as she caressed his cheek. Gil reached for her, and when he gingerly laid his hand on her back, he didn't have to pull her close. Her body just seemed to melt against his of its own accord.

'And this?'

She nodded.

'I can't think how I could have forgotten...'

Right now it seemed that this moment would stay in his memory for ever.

'I...wasn't sure how to tell you.' She looked up at him, twisting the corners of her mouth down.

She should never do that. Gil didn't want to ever make her regret anything. He leaned down, to drop a kiss on the side of her mouth and smooth away the frown. She shifted in his arms, turning her lips towards his, kissing him.

This time, he couldn't bear to let her go. She was so sweet, and yet so passionate, stirring the echoes of what felt like a long-lost memory, but in truth was just a part of a dream. One of those dreams about the ideal woman that no one ever expected to find. Somehow he'd managed to find Clemmie twice...

And then she broke away from him. Had he done the wrong thing?

'How about those cappuccino cocktails? We could always get back to this later...' Her smile told him that kissing her had been exactly the right thing.

And now she was doing the right thing, too. It gave him a bit of time to process the sudden shift in their relationship, and how he felt about it. And something to do while he was processing...

Gil walked over to the kitchen dresser, opening the top cupboard and reaching for the drink bottles. 'Can you remember the proportions?'

'I think so. You make the coffee and we'll see if I get it right. I know that Kahlua is the main one.'

Gil nodded, flipping the switch for the coffee maker and fetching ice from the freezer to cool the mixture. Watching her examine the bottles and line them up in order of importance on the counter. Order, amongst all the chaos that was pounding in his heart.

'Don't tell me…' She smiled up at him, studying the bottles carefully and then rearranging them. Gil shook his head and she looked at the bottles again, swapping two of them around.

'Interesting.' He grinned down at her. She'd remembered that Kahlua was the principal ingredient, but got some of the others mixed up.

'That means it's not *quite* the same as your recipe.'

Gil shrugged. 'Maybe it'll be better.'

'Let's see, shall we?'

Gil reached for the cocktail shaker and handed it to her. Clemmie carefully measured out the spirits, and then poured the iced coffee onto the mix.

She poured the mixture into glasses, adding the ice-cold milk that he'd frothed. Then he led her back outside, to sit in the warm scent of the evening air.

'Here goes...' She clinked her glass against his and took a sip. 'Not bad.'

Gil tried his. 'Not bad at all. In fact, with a bit more Kahlua I think it's better than mine.'

Clemmie grinned. 'We'll have to try that another time.'

Another time... Gil smiled. She'd just widened everything out, so that everything didn't depend on this moment. This night. She'd allowed him the time to come to terms with a relationship with someone who he knew so little about, but who knew so much about him.

'Another time. Yeah...' Suddenly he didn't need more time. He could trust Clemmie to let him know whatever he needed to know. He leaned back in his seat, savouring the moment as it swirled around him in the gathering darkness.

But it was slipping away. Clemmie had finished her drink and they'd sat for a while enjoying the warm silence of the evening, but now she was sliding towards the edge of her seat. Using that body language that announced that she was about to go and leave him alone with his thoughts. The ones that only included her.

'It's been a good day, Gil. I hope we can do this again.'

Maybe he should wait. But having Clemmie here with him in his home felt so different from being with her at work. He couldn't quite fathom why...

Then it hit him. Everything they'd done and said at work had been centred around how they'd felt seven years ago. Here, surrounded by the everyday and without constant reminders of the fallout from brain injury, it was all about how they felt now.

When Clemmie got to her feet, he saw a fleeting moment of regret on her face. She felt it too, that freedom from the chains of the past. It was all he needed to know, and he rose, taking her into his arms.

What might have been a kiss goodnight turned into something much, much more. Something that burned into him, a beginning rather than an ending.

'I'd love it if...you stayed a little longer.' He tried not to put too many expectations into his words.

She smiled, her eyes dark in the failing light. 'On our first date?'

That was the heart of it. 'My first. I can live with that if you can.'

'Since it's not my first, I can make an exception.' She reached up, her fingers tracing his cheek. 'No expectations, eh?'

'I have little to base any expectations on.'

Clemmie kissed him again, and made him into a liar. Her kiss let him know exactly what to expect from this evening, and it was all good.

Clemmie had resisted this for so long. And yet now that the time had come, it was so easy to do. Maybe they could break that final boundary and be together. Not just ignore the secrets of the past, but come to terms with them…

She shivered suddenly in response to the thought, and Gil stilled. Waiting for her to say something, but she wasn't sure what to say. She wanted him so much, but Gil's honest gaze deserved her honesty in return.

'It's okay. Whatever you're thinking.' Gil's murmured words gave her strength. Maybe it *was* okay.

'I…' Clemmie took a deep breath, looking up into his eyes. 'There was someone else. After I met you…'

He nodded. 'You owed me nothing, Clemmie. You thought I'd deserted you.'

All the same, she should tell him now. Maybe leave out the parts that made it obvious she'd fallen into Harry's arms as a result of Gil's actions…

'You need to know that—' She fell silent as he laid his finger across her lips.

'Let me tell you what I need to know. Was there someone else when we were together?'

Clemmie smiled at the thought. 'Seriously, Gil? There was no time for anything or anyone else.'

'Sounds as if we had our priorities straight.' He gave her a wicked smile. 'Is there anyone else now?'

That was an easy question, as well. 'No.'

'It's the same for me. There was no one else then, and there isn't now. If you want to know more, I can tell you about the couple of brief flirtations in between, that never went anywhere.'

Clemmie shook her head. 'I don't need to know. I'm glad you weren't lonely.'

'I was lonely. When I found you, I realised why that was. I think that even though I didn't remember you, I always knew that there was something missing.'

That was more than enough information. Clemmie kissed him and he responded with a new hunger. This time, his hands didn't shake when he touched her. It was a lot for someone to deal with, but it seemed that Gil had come to terms with it all a little quicker than she'd imagined he would, and in exactly the way she wanted him to.

No expectations.

That was hard, because she couldn't help wanting this to be the same as it had been last time. But Gil was a changed man, in so many ways. Not so driven, and without that brash confidence that had allowed him to challenge her so deliciously.

And then he made *that* move. The one that she'd loved so much, the one that made her feel as if she were the one and only person in his world. Seen and heard, and capable of so much more than she'd thought. One arm coiled around her waist, pulling her tight against him. Gil was staring down at her, the fingers of his other hand caressing her face, his kisses following their path. Watching her closely, his lips curving into a smile when she sighed her approval. All hers…

And she knew exactly what he wanted. He'd never seemed to tire of exploring her body, how it fitted with his and every way that she reacted to his caress. When she pulled away from him, she saw self-doubt in his face, but when she took his hands in hers and guided him back through the open door and into the darkened sitting room, he smiled.

'Clemmie…?'

She pushed him down onto the sofa, silencing him with a finger across his lips. Two silhouettes, taking their time to renew what had once been everything.

As she began to unbutton her dress, he leaned to one side, reaching to switch on the lamp.

'You're far too beautiful to do this in the dark.'

It was how he made her feel. How his gaze made her feel, following each and every movement she made. Making her hands shake as she slipped the soft fabric from her shoulders. He gave her all the confidence she needed to walk slowly towards him, climbing onto his lap, her legs astride his.

'Clemmie... Please talk to me...'

'Don't you know what comes next?' She started to unbutton his shirt and he grinned.

'I have a good idea. I guess you already know I like to play a little first.'

'So do I.' She leaned forward, kissing his cheek. 'Am I going too fast for you?'

He shook his head. 'You have perfect timing. But I need you to talk to me. Tell me what you're feeling.'

What she was feeling had always been so important to him, and that was what had bound them together, in a way that Clemmie had never experienced with anyone else. He'd seemed to know instinctively, but of course it had been the result of watching and listening. Gil did that so well that it had seemed effortless.

'Take all the time you need to catch up. In fact, I insist that you do.' Her lips brushed his ear as she whispered, 'I want to see a little more of you.'

He was still there. The Gil that didn't know what else to do with a challenge other than meet it head-on. He leaned forward, so that she could pull his shirt off, and then back again, his fingers running lightly across her body. *Now* she could say it. In the heat of a warm night, she could tell him all of the things that she liked best, whispering them into his ear without needing to mince her words. And he followed through, doing everything that she asked of him.

'Did you do this before? Telling me exactly what you want?' He grinned, acceding to her request to unfasten the catch on her bra.

'No. You like it?'

'Very much. Particularly the finer details.' His hand covered her breast, the thumb brushing the nipple in a move all of his own. 'You?'

'You don't need to ask that, do you?' Clemmie had already shown him how much she liked this intimate conversation.

'I guess not.'

'Then do it again...'

Gil chuckled. 'Like this?'

She was beyond telling him now, but her sigh was enough of an answer. He lifted her against him, kissing her breasts until Clemmie groaned with the sweet agony of it all. 'Stop…please. You're going to make me come…'

'That would be a bad thing?' He let her sink back down onto his lap.

'It would be, if I didn't have you inside me.'

'I was hoping you might say that.' He kissed her, sliding forward in his seat and lifting her up in his arms. 'You want to go upstairs?'

'Yes.' All she wanted now, after this long and delicious foreplay, was to dispense with words. Have him take her in all the ways he'd taken her before.

Gil carried her upstairs. The bedroom was lit only by moonlight, slanting in through the windows and across her body when he laid her down on the bed. He swiftly closed the curtains, leaving the door open so that light from the hallway could illuminate the room.

Clemmie watched as he undressed. His body was still the same. Strong and immeasurably beautiful. And he still hesitated for a moment, one hand brushing his chest as if he was in some doubt about whether she liked what she saw. He'd done that the last time, taking nothing for granted.

'Come here, Gil.'

He took a moment to open one of the drawers in the dresser and take out a pack of condoms, and then he did as he was told. Batting her hands away when she tried to remove her briefs, so that he could do it himself. They were beyond words now, each knowing that all they wanted was to be finally together.

She cried out as he slid gently inside her. Then again, as he lifted one of her legs, pushing further. Clemmie closed her eyes, gritting her teeth, trying to make this last just a little longer.

He stilled suddenly, leaving her in an agony of frustrated desire. 'Open your eyes, Clemmie.'

When she did so, she could see that he too was very close to the edge. But even now, the most important thing to Gil was that they should keep the bond that had grown again so naturally between them, and that they should make love staring into each other's eyes.

'Now let go.'

Did she dare? After everything that had happened? There was really no choice in the matter, because every instinct was telling her that she wanted to feel what he'd do when she did.

'Take me with you, Gil. Wherever you want us to go.'

He nodded, rolling them both onto their sides.

Lifting his weight from her leg, and then twisting his body, so that when he slid inside her again the angle was different. A little less friction, but much more depth, and his free hand was able to reach any part of her body.

Gil was calculated and precise. He made it last until he'd told her everything that was on his mind, how beautiful she was and how much he loved everything they were doing. Building her up so that when the orgasm came it was so strong that it might have shaken them apart, if he hadn't been holding on to her so tight.

And then his. She felt him stiffen and swell inside her, and then give himself to her with a helpless roar of feeling. It felt better than it had before, because now they knew each other in ways they hadn't when they'd first met. They were no longer just charmed lovers… They'd had to forgive each other and build this new relationship from the ruins of the old.

She snuggled into his arms, and he covered them with the light duvet that lay on the end of the bed. Holding on to him so that maybe she'd figure in his dreams.

'You okay?' Clemmie felt him kiss the top of her head.

'No. I'm a lot better than that.'

'Me too.' He hugged her and Clemmie lay quietly by his side. His fingers brushed her shoulder, and he shifted a little closer. 'You're sure? You're very quiet…'

'Don't you want—?' Clemmie stopped herself. 'You don't want to sleep, do you?'

'That's not number one on my list of priorities. Why…?' He puffed out a breath. 'You're telling me that the last time we did this, I just rolled over and went to sleep afterwards, aren't you?'

'You were very tired. You said you'd been working some long shifts before you arrived at the conference.'

'Don't make excuses for me. You *are* telling me that I went to sleep.'

'I didn't mind. I liked watching you sleep.' Clemmie propped herself up on her elbow and saw the pained look on Gil's face.

'Don't. I can't believe that you didn't kick me out of bed for falling asleep on you.'

'We were in your hotel room, so it would have been difficult. Anyway, you're very cute when you're asleep.'

'Always good to know.' He rolled over, covering her body with his. Holding her so tenderly that it felt she was melting into him again. 'And maybe you were a bit more accepting of bad behaviour in others then.'

There were some things that Gil didn't need

to be told; he just saw and understood them. But he was wrong about this.

'It didn't seem so surprising to me that people would ignore what I wanted.' She shook her head when he went to protest. 'You were the one who challenged that and made me understand what it was like to be seen. We've both changed, Gil.'

'I'm not so stressed out and tired, and you're comfortable with telling me what you want.'

Comfortable wasn't the word for it. Telling Gil what she'd wanted and having him respond to that had been exhilarating. 'Don't you know that already?'

He bent to kiss her. 'I loved it, too. So much that I'm going to demand you do it again. You can go to sleep, or... Strawberries maybe? A back massage?'

'Can I have both?'

He grinned, disentangling himself from her arms and pulling on a pair of jogging bottoms. 'That'll be my pleasure...'

Gil was trying so hard to make it all up to her. He didn't need to. All he really needed to do was to be the same man who saw her and heard her, and who she'd fallen in love with the first time around. They could leave all the hurt between them where it belonged, in a past that he didn't remember.

CHAPTER ELEVEN

CLEMMIE HAD STAYED until Sunday evening. It had been wonderful, something that Gil hadn't been able to hope could ever happen. But it had, and it was better than he could have ever imagined. They'd walked down to a small restaurant for lunch, sitting outside. Tables and chairs stretched out across the cobbled street, which was closed on Sundays to make a pedestrian walkway that buzzed with life. Then they'd gone home and made love again. Gil was beginning to wonder whether this was all he'd ever need out of life. Good food, the warmth of the sun, and Clemmie. The first two reminded him of Australia, and Clemmie reminded him of everything that felt right in the world.

It was no surprise that it couldn't last. After she'd gone home, to prepare for the week's work ahead of them, Gil had sat alone in the garden. In the quiet of the evening, doubts buzzed around him like mosquitoes.

There was so much she hadn't told him. Would she ever have admitted that they'd slept together if it hadn't been for the cappuccino cocktails? The drip-feed of information was like a leaking tap. You could lie awake all night waiting for the sound of the next splash of water.

He knew how hard this had been for Clemmie. And he didn't blame her for keeping things back; she'd found herself in an impossible situation. The thing that worried him the most was that she'd kept the things back that she knew would hurt him. The things he'd done that made his head and his heart throb with guilt.

But he couldn't let her go now. When they made love, he knew that she was holding nothing back from him. In time, everything else would follow.

He went to bed early, and her scent on the pillow was enough to lull him into a deep, dreamless sleep. In the morning, he took his bike from the lean-to in the garden. It had been a couple of weeks since he'd gone for a long ride, and that always cleared his head. A turn around the cycle paths in Richmond Park was what he needed, and there was plenty of time before he needed to be at work.

'Been for a swim?' Gil's hair was still wet when Jahira appeared in the doorway of his office.

'A shower. I cycled to work this morning. What are you doing here, Jahira?' Patients weren't barred from any part of the unit, but they very seldom came to the part of the building that housed the offices.

'I want to ask you something.'

'Okay. Come in and take a seat.' Jahira was hanging on to the door handle to steady herself and Gil got up to offer his arm. She shot him a ferocious look.

'What's the point of me walking all the way here by myself, if you're going to go and spoil it?'

Gil chuckled. 'Sorry. You made it from your room to here without your walking frame?'

'Yep.' Jahira walked unsteadily across the room, sitting down in a visitor's chair with a bump.

Now probably wasn't the time to remind her that she shouldn't overdo it and fall. Gil sat down in the other visitor's chair and gave her a smile. 'Nice job. I'm really impressed.'

Jahira grinned. 'Yeah. I'm a bit puffed now.'

'So how's your memory book going?' Clemmie had shown him various bits and pieces, sparkly stars and hearts, and a sheet of beautiful hand-printed paper that she'd gone out to buy one lunchtime, and Jahira had explained to him exactly what the empty album on her desk would contain.

'Good. Sarah's learning a few things about me. My mum brought in a load of photos from when I was a kid.'

Jahira was still just a kid; she was only seventeen. But she was learning to shape her own life again, and see where she fitted in with the people that she loved. It was a process that never failed to inspire Gil, because everyone did it differently.

'That sounds great. Will you show it to me when it's done?'

Jahira nodded.

'So what did you come to see me for?' Gil prompted her. 'Assuming it wasn't just to show off about how far you can walk, that is.'

'Oh. No, it wasn't. I've got a problem. It's Edward.'

'Okay. Tell me about it.' Gil wondered if the two of them had fallen out.

'He's got a girlfriend.' Jahira frowned, obviously reconsidering the word. Gil gave her a moment.

'A lady friend?'

'Yeah. She's a senior citizen. And Edward really fancies her. His wife died, you know.'

'Yes, I'm aware. How do you know all this, Jahira?' Gil almost didn't like to ask.

'Because he introduced me to her when she came. He had his best waistcoat on, and I'm sure he was wearing aftershave. I know he wants to take her out, but he can't. He's proud.'

The speech therapist was clearly making great strides with Jahira. For one moment Gil wished that the girl had decided to express herself on a different subject and then dismissed the thought. He'd seen Edward helping Jahira in the garden, talking to her when she became frustrated with her efforts to pick up the small seeds she'd spilled on the table. Jahira was trying to do something nice for her new friend, and this was exactly the kind of thing that he encouraged here. Everyone helping everyone else.

'Okay. You have something in mind?'

Jahira nodded. 'We could put a table in the garden and make them tea and cakes. Like a date.'

It wasn't such a bad idea, at that. The walled garden would be perfect, and Gil knew that although Edward made a point of never complaining, he felt the loss of his independence keenly. A treat for his lady friend might be just the thing he needed.

'It's a kind idea, Jahira, but we have to make sure that Edward really wants us to do something like this, so you're going to have to ask him. Take Clemmie with you.'

Jahira nodded. 'Yeah, Clemmie will know what to say. I can bake a cake if you like. My mum's got lots of recipes.'

'That sounds really nice. But first of all we'll ask Edward, shall we?'

'Okay. Thanks.'

'My pleasure. Would you like to go back to the lounge now? I'll ask Clemmie to come and see you as soon as she gets here.'

Jahira nodded, getting to her feet and taking Gil's arm. The effort of getting here had clearly taken some toll—she was leaning on him—and Gil made a mental note to mention to the physiotherapist that Jahira's enthusiasm sometimes outstripped her capabilities.

'You've got a bike, then. You'd better tell me that you wear a cycle helmet.'

Jahira's words came right out of the blue. Her own injury had been caused by colliding with a car while cycling to college, and her parents had told Gil that it had been the one morning that she hadn't worn a cycle helmet.

'Yes, I do. Thank you for reminding me.'

'Can I see it? Your bike.'

'You can't ride it, if that's what you're asking. Your balance isn't good enough yet.' And getting back onto a bike might be more difficult than Jahira imagined. Gil understood her impatience, he'd felt that same impatience himself, but it was important that she didn't try to do too much, too soon.

'I don't want to ride it.' Jahira pressed her lips together. 'I think I'd like to just look at it, though.'

'Okay, that's fine. Today's a bit booked up but I'll bring it in tomorrow, and you can look at it all you like.' Perhaps he would mention the idea to Jahira's mother first, just to make sure.

'Thanks. Edward says that when you mess up with something, you have to take a breath and try again.'

It was good advice, although Edward had probably been talking about spilled seeds at the time. Maybe Gil should heed it himself. Giving up on Clemmie because *he'd* messed up didn't seem fair. He had to face his own mistakes and shortcomings, and deal with them.

'Yeah, he's right. But sometimes, with the big things, you have to give yourself a bit of time.'

When he arrived back in his office, Clemmie was sitting in one of the visitors' chairs. He closed the door behind him, walking behind his desk and sitting down. He didn't dare get too close. Even the desk between them was fast becoming a temptation…

He needed to get a grip. Avoiding horizontal surfaces while in her presence wasn't going to be practical. Clemmie had that mischievous smile on her face that he adored so much and he couldn't help grinning back at her.

He held out as long as he could, staring into her eyes, and finally she broke. Her hand flew to her mouth as she started to giggle, and Gil began to laugh, too.

'So we did it, then.' The look on her face left Gil in no doubt about how she felt about that.

'Yeah, we did.' Gil could almost feel the touch of her lips on his, still. 'You look beautiful today.'

'So do you.' She lowered her gaze suddenly. 'I'm sorry I didn't tell you.'

'Hey.' He wanted so badly to reach out to her, but when Clemmie looked up at him, being caught in her gaze seemed a good second best. 'I know why you didn't tell me. You didn't want me to know how much I'd hurt you.'

'You didn't mean to, Gil.'

'No, I didn't. That doesn't make me feel any better about it, but that's for me to deal with.' Now that she was here, Gil didn't want to talk about how guilty he felt. He just wanted to see her smile again.

'We can put it behind us?'

He couldn't deny her anything. 'Yeah. The future's a nicer place than the past.'

'Thank you.' She smiled suddenly and Gil promptly forgot that anything else existed.

'There's a new tea shop in the town centre. Want to come and try it out with me at lunchtime?'

'A date?'

'More a working lunch. I thought we might leave the date until this evening.'

Clemmie's smile broadened. 'That sounds perfect, Gil. I can't wait.'

'Me neither.' They didn't need to rush things, this time. They had a second chance, and Gil wanted to make it work, however difficult it had all seemed last night. This morning it didn't feel so much of a mountain to climb.

'So what's on the agenda for today? While we're both looking forward to our date tonight?'

'Would you believe another date? I was talking to Jahira just now, and she's had an idea…'

Clemmie had been juggling several different projects in the last week, but she'd arranged everything. She'd decided that Edward should wait in the garden for his lady friend, Caroline, and so Maggie was put on alert to watch for her arrival. There had been activity in the kitchen, which Gil had largely been excluded from, and Jahira was bubbling with excitement. Clemmie had made sure that Edward was looking extra-smart today, and wheeled him out to the garden to sit under a large sunshade, at a table with fresh white linen and silver cutlery that she'd borrowed from somewhere and brought in.

'I don't know about this.' Gil had decided to keep Edward company while he waited, and it seemed that he had last-minute nerves.

'She'll love it.'

Edward surveyed the table in front of him. 'I don't have much to offer her.'

Edward wasn't much of a talker, usually buckling down and getting on with whatever task presented itself. He was clearly very nervous.

'I can relate to that.'

Edward glanced up at him. 'Jahira told me that you were in here, some time ago. With a brain injury like hers.'

'Yes, that's right.'

'Young fellow like you shouldn't have any difficulty with the ladies, though.' Edward raised an eyebrow.

'That's not the point. I looked at what I'd been before the injury, and I reckoned I'd never be the same again.' Gil wondered whether Clemmie would mind him saying a bit more, and decided that she'd be cross with him if he didn't.

'For a long time I thought that no woman would accept me the way I was. But I've met someone, and she's made it perfectly clear to me that she would have accepted me then, the same way she does now.'

Edward smiled. The same kind of lopsided smile that Gil had been able to offer, and he could see now that was enough. Edward was perceptive and kind, he could talk about all manner of things and places he'd seen in the course of his career, and he was a gentleman. He had a great deal to offer.

'Good show. That's one thing you can say about the ladies. We're none of us good enough for them, but they don't seem to mind about that.'

Gil chuckled. 'No, they don't.'

'Just as well, I suppose,' Edward mused, seeming a little happier about the prospect of his afternoon tea.

They didn't have too long to wait. Caroline had arrived promptly at the appointed time. Gil saw Maggie, who had deserted her post for once, at the back door of the clinic, pointing the way to the walled garden. Carrying a bag that was no doubt stuffed with things she'd brought for Edward, Caroline walked along the path towards them.

'Here goes nothing,' Edward muttered under his breath, and Gil got to his feet, leaving him alone to face what was probably one of the biggest challenges he'd meet here. It went against the grain, but Clemmie had been adamant that Edward should greet Caroline on his own.

Jahira was hidden behind a spreading rhododendron that stood on the outer side of the wall. She looked just as nervous as Edward.

'What if I made a mistake? What if she just wants to be his friend?'

'Then it's a nice tea on a sunny afternoon. What's not to like about that?'

Jahira shot him an annoyed look. 'You really don't understand, do you?'

Gil understood, better than Jahira could imagine. He still had mixed feelings about whether he'd ever been good enough for Clemmie, but now wasn't the time to share them.

'It's all set now. You'd better call Clemmie.'

Jahira nodded, pulling her phone from her pocket and fumbling with it. She could manage autodial now, but her nerves were making it difficult. Gil resisted the instinct to help her, knowing that doing things for herself was a lot more valuable to Jahira.

'What's happening?' A woman's voice sounded

from the other side of the wall, and Jahira stiffened. Gil stretched up, peeping over, and smiled.

Edward had made it to his feet when Caroline arrived, and Gil mentally congratulated the physio for working so hard with him to make that possible. Caroline was standing, her hands over her mouth, obviously thrilled. Edward made a gesture towards the chair that had been set opposite him and waited for Caroline to sit down before he lowered himself back into his seat.

'We're good. She's sitting down and she looks really pleased.' Gil was starting to feel excited now.

'What are they saying?'

'I can't hear. Come along—you're up now. And take your walker.'

Jahira pulled a face and grabbed the walker, the two menus that Clemmie had printed out in the basket that was fixed to the front of it. Clemmie had worked her magic with Jahira as well, helping her to plait her hair in a complicated, one-sided arrangement that made the shaved side of her head look as if it were a fashion statement, and choosing a bright top for her to wear.

As expected, Jahira abandoned the walker as soon as she got to the entrance of the garden and walked the last few yards on her own. She delivered the menus to Edward, who handed one to Caroline. Then Edward gestured to an empty chair and Jahira sat down.

Okay, so that wasn't part of the plan. But Caroline was studying her menu carefully and smiling, and Edward was talking now, looking far more relaxed. If it worked, it worked.

Clemmie appeared, walking out from the back of the building carrying a laden tray, and his heart lifted, the way it always did when he saw her. Reckoning that the little group in the garden would be all right for a few minutes on their own, he went to meet her, relieving the cook who was following of her tray.

'How's it going?'

'Okay so far. She looks pleased.'

'Oh, well, that's a good sign, eh?' Clemmie grinned up at him, her usual optimism breaking through and calming Gil's own fears.

They carried the trays into the garden. Clemmie had found a cake stand from somewhere, and arranged sandwiches and scones on it, along with two slices of the delicious-looking cake that Jahira and her mother had made together, in the rehab centre's kitchen. There were little tubs of cream and jam for the scones, and a good supply of napkins, in case Edward's shaking hand made any mess. On Gil's tray, two pretty china cups and a matching teapot, with a tea cosy.

'This is wonderful. Thank you so much!' Caroline exclaimed.

'Edward's our friend, so we helped him do it for you.' Jahira grinned.

Gil had been hoping that Jahira wouldn't say the wrong thing, but he'd underestimated her. It was exactly the right thing to say and Caroline beamed at Edward.

Clemmie finished unloading the trays and poured the tea. Edward added milk, using his good hand, and pushed one of the cups across the table to Caroline, who picked it up and took a sip, then nodded her approval to Edward.

'You have everything?' Clemmie took her phone out of her pocket and put it down on the table next to Edward. 'Maggie's on speed dial, and if you call her when you've finished, she'll get hold of me.'

'Thank you.' Edward gave Clemmie a look that made all of this worthwhile, and she smiled back at him, grabbing Jahira's hand and coaxing her to her feet to leave the couple alone now.

'You think they'll be okay?' Clemmie asked as she and Gil walked away.

'With half the unit watching out of the windows, and Jahira standing guard outside? I can't see what could happen to them.'

Clemmie's elbow found his ribs. 'That's not what I mean. Where's your instinct for romance?'

Gil chuckled. 'If you don't know by now, I'll have to try a little harder.'

'You're fine, just as you are. I think Edward will be, too.'

CHAPTER TWELVE

CLEMMIE HAD STAYED LATE, to catch Jahira's mother when she came to visit that evening. The afternoon tea had been everything she'd hoped it would, and Edward had confided afterwards that he'd suggested that he and Caroline might see a little more of each other when he came home from rehab. To his surprise and relief, she'd replied in the affirmative, wanting to know why on earth it had taken him so long to ask.

Clemmie walked back to Gil's house. He'd be home already, after having grabbed up some paperwork that he'd said he needed some peace and quiet to finish. Clemmie hoped that he'd be done by now, and that the rest of the evening would be theirs to enjoy.

He was sitting in the garden, staring out at the apple trees. Clemmie sat down with him and he turned, smiling.

'Got all your pruning sorted out in your head?'

'That's not going to be until February. It gives them a chance to grow after you've cut the dead wood back.'

'So what's up, then?' Something was obviously bothering him. 'Edward's over the moon. When I left he was polishing off the rest of the cake with Jahira and her mum.'

'That's nice.'

There was something in his eyes. A longing that matched her own, along with regret.

'What's up, Gil?'

He heaved a sigh. 'Do you ever wonder? What might have happened if I hadn't had the brain bleed. If I'd called you.'

There was a whole weight of sadness and mistakes in that seven years. Clemmie nodded. 'Yes, I wonder.'

'I know that you didn't want to talk about that, Clemmie. But our relationship's changing. I love that it is, but it makes for different boundaries.'

He was right. Being with Gil was wonderful, but there was more to talk about. Clemmie would have to choose her words very carefully.

'It's difficult.'

He nodded. Maybe he'd decided that it was all too difficult. There were risks involved in telling him more, but the last week had taught Clemmie just how much she wanted the reward.

'I guess we both need a push.' She looked at him hopefully. Gil hadn't let her down yet, and she couldn't imagine a situation where he could.

'I guess we do. Something pushed me today.'

Suddenly he got to his feet, walking into the house. He reappeared moments later, holding a brown paper bag, folded over at the top.

'What's that?' Gil put the bag down on the table and she peered inside. He'd been to the handmade chocolate shop and bought her favourite truffles. 'Are they for me?'

Gil chuckled. 'You know they are. Not yet, though…'

Clemmie took her hand guiltily out of the bag. 'You're right. After we've talked…'

He shot her an unfathomable look, sitting down opposite her. 'Truth or Dare, Clemmie. You want to play?'

Clemmie raised her eyebrows. 'With chocolate?'

He nodded.

'Gil, have you actually ever played Truth or Dare before? You're not supposed to reward someone with chocolate if they decide not to tell the truth.'

'I've played it. Think about it this way. If I don't tell you the truth, then I'll have to eat one of them, which means that's one less for you. Which I'm not prepared to contemplate, because I love watching the look on your face when you eat truffles. If, on the other hand, you decide not to tell the truth, then you don't have too onerous a dare. That's working pretty well for me as a concept.'

He'd been listening, to all she'd said. He knew that she wasn't finding it easy to be the one who remembered when he didn't, and he was giving her a way out. She might take it if she needed it, but she wanted this chance to share more.

'So you're planning on telling the truth, without expecting me to do the same.' Clemmie pushed the bag away from her into the centre of the table. 'I think you underestimate the effect that chocolate has on me, Gil. It's far more likely to loosen my tongue than tequila shots.'

'Then perhaps this is a bad idea.'

He reached for the bag and Clemmie laid her trembling fingers on his. The one thing she knew for sure was that Gil wouldn't hurt her. It was only the secrets that could do that, and if they were ever going to move forward, perhaps some of those secrets needed to be told.

'It's not a bad idea at all. Can I go first?'

He nodded. 'Of course.'

Clemmie thought hard.

'What happened today? To push you?'

'I was talking to Edward and he said that he didn't have much to offer Caroline.' He started to answer without any hesitation. 'It made me think, because I felt that way after my TBI. I could have called you a lot earlier than I did, but I looked at the photo and you were so beautiful and full of life... I put it off, and by the time I was at a point where I felt that I did have something to offer, it was too late.'

Clemmie took a deep breath. It hurt, but knowing the reason why was helping her to understand. 'I would have taken you, Gil. Any way you were.'

He nodded. 'I know. I told Edward as much.'

'Good. That was one piece of good advice for him, at least.' Clemmie couldn't leave it there. 'Supplementary question?'

He nodded. 'Be my guest.'

'How do you feel about that?'

That was harder for him to answer, and Gil paused for a moment.

'Guilty. Full of regret.'

'You shouldn't. I understand—' Gil held his hand up to stop her.

'You asked how I felt and I told you. There's no blame here, just the truth.'

That was reassuring. Clemmie reckoned that Gil might have some awkward questions for her, and this 'no blame' policy would certainly work in her favour.

'Okay. Your turn.'

He thought for a moment. 'When we were first together. There was something you wanted to tell me.'

Cold fingers of panic squeezed Clemmie's heart. 'You said you didn't need to know.'

'I didn't. I don't now. It's none of my business. It seemed important to you at the time, and I wonder if it's still important now.'

Clemmie grabbed the bag of chocolates and Gil reached out, putting his hand over hers.

'That's probably an unfair question. Take a pass on the dare.'

Clemmie rolled her eyes. 'You really *don't* know how chocolate works, do you, Gil?' She unwrapped one of the truffles, putting it into her mouth. 'I want to tell you.'

He nodded, taking the bag from her, a quiet smile hovering around his lips. Okay, so he wanted to make sure it wasn't just the chocolate talking. Probably wise—she could have eaten a few more of these.

'I was married for a short while. It only lasted for eighteen months and...' She shot him a pleading look. It was past time that she told him, but that didn't make it any easier.

'It's been seven years. I'd be shocked to hear

that you hadn't had a life.' Gil seemed to be taking the news well.

'Harry and I were at school together. He had a bit of a crush on me when we were in the sixth form, but I made it clear that all I was interested in was friendship. I thought he knew that, but...' Clemmie shrugged. Harry had renewed his interest in her at just about the time she'd realised that Gil wasn't going to phone. Maybe he'd sensed her sadness and vulnerability. But Gil must never know that.

He nodded. Waiting.

'It was a bit of a whirlwind thing. Harry was determined it was the right thing for us and I should have listened to my doubts.'

'Why didn't you?'

Clemmie shrugged. 'I needed an anchor, something stable. Harry was so attentive, so sure about everything, and I was grateful to him for that. I thought it was love. But all he was really seeing was someone who would reflect what he wanted. Harry could be very manipulative in getting what he wanted, and I found out that it had been a deliberate thing on his part. We separated and the divorce came through earlier this year.'

'I'm sorry that he made you unhappy. You deserve more, Clemmie.'

Clemmie reached out, putting her hand in

his, and he wound his fingers around hers. So warm and reassuring. It was possible to forget that she hadn't told Gil the one secret that she knew would really hurt him. That she'd married Harry because of the way that Gil had broken her heart.

'Thanks for understanding.'

'I don't, not really. I don't understand how someone could try to control you, when you're perfectly capable of ordering your own life. But I'm hoping you made that very clear to him.'

Clemmie smiled. Gil's protectiveness wasn't the rigid, controlling kind that Harry had demonstrated. 'Yes, I did. When I finally came to my senses.'

He squeezed her hand, seeming to forget all about truths or dares. Warmth ignited in his eyes and it would be so easy to leave this conversation where it was and start another very different conversation. The intimate give and take of their lovemaking.

But she'd started and she wanted to finish. 'Harry made things very difficult after I left him—it was as if any contact was better than nothing, even if it was conflict. He haggled over everything that I hadn't been able to squeeze into my suitcase, even my clothes. He emptied out our joint bank account and I had nothing. I went to see my parents and they let me stay with them for a few months. But my mum kept asking me whether I was ready to go back home to Harry yet. She just couldn't see that it wasn't my home and that it never really had been.'

'She didn't see how you really felt. Didn't see *you*.' Gil unerringly picked up on the point of what Clemmie was trying to say.

'No. A few of my friends clubbed together and lent me the cash for a deposit on a bedsit. It wasn't much but it was mine. When I got the money to pay them back, they wouldn't take it. They said that they were glad to see me away from Harry, and that I was to put the money towards a mortgage.'

'I'm glad you had someone to support you. You have your own place now?'

'Yes. I don't have much furniture…' Clemmie grinned at him. 'That's why I haven't asked you over.'

'I was wondering. I'd like to come and visit you, if that's all right.'

'I might put you to work. There's a lot to do still.'

'That would be my pleasure. Supplementary question?'

Clemmie nodded.

'How do you feel now? About being seen and heard. It seems that your parents really let you down, and that must have been a crushing blow.'

'To be honest, they did more than I expected them to. But I've made choices, and I've built a new life. It's my choice to be with you now, Gil, and one of the reasons for that is that you do see and hear me.'

He leaned across the table, kissing her. 'Always, Clemmie. Seeing you and hearing you is the best part of my day.'

'Can we leave it behind, Gil? Everything that's happened?' That was really the only question that Clemmie needed to ask.

'I wouldn't be here if I didn't think so.' He answered without hesitation.

She shifted from her seat, rounding the table and sitting back down on his lap. Gil wound his arms around her, holding her tenderly. Something had changed, and it had changed for the better. The secrets and the lost time were starting to be acknowledged, and Gil's understanding was weakening their hold.

'Are you done with this game?' He kissed her.

'I'm really glad we talked.' Clemmie kissed him back. 'And yes, I'm done with it for the moment.'

'Good.' He reached for the bag of truffles.

'Because I'd really like you to explain to me exactly how chocolate works for you…'

There had been something different in their lovemaking. It was no longer a way of forgetting all that had happened between them, but of celebrating their bond and strengthening it.

Gil had made a late-night snack, because they'd missed dinner completely. Clemmie sat cross-legged on one of the chairs on the patio, wearing only one of his shirts. She looked great in any outfit, but that was the one he liked the best. The stray smudge of chocolate on the collar was a great accessory.

'Can I ask you another question?'

'You make that sound as if I have the ability to say no to you.'

'It's always an option.'

Yeah. Dressed like that, and with the sweet remembrance of her caress still on his skin. Clemmie really did underestimate herself.

'Ask away.'

'What about your family? I'm not close to my mum and dad now, but we did at least have a chance to repair the relationship, even if it didn't work out. It's not so easy for you, with your family in Australia.'

'It's hard to sort things out when you're depending on phone calls. But it's better. I talk a bit more and so do my mum and dad. When Mum yelled at me for not telling her about the TBI sooner, it was a bit of a wake-up call.'

Clemmie smiled. 'That's nice. That she yelled.'

'Yeah, it was.' It had been the start of a change in their relationship, which had allowed some admission of frailty, even if Gil still tended to gloss over any difficulties he had in life.

'They're mellowing a bit as they get older. My dad retired last year, to everyone's surprise. He's substituted hobbies for work, and he pursues them pretty relentlessly, but there's something about sitting on a boat and dangling a fishing line into the ocean that defies too much stress.'

'Even if they're big fish?' Clemmie's eyes widened.

'They're big fish.' Gil held out his hands to indicate the size and her eyebrows flew up. 'There's quite a bit of competition about who can catch the biggest, but there's still that element of going and catching what you eat that keeps him grounded. A bit like growing what you eat, only strawberry plants don't usually put up so much of a struggle.'

'It sounds as if you have a better relationship with them now.'

Gil shrugged. 'I've never really had a *bad*

relationship with them. Just a little dysfunctional maybe.'

Clemmie took a deep breath. Clearly she had something on her mind. 'Will you do me a favour?'

'Depends what it is…' Gil returned Clemmie's steady gaze. He really couldn't deny her anything. 'Strike that. The answer's yes.'

'Will you go and see them? Or at least call them and start a dialogue. Let them know if you're in a bit of a jam.'

Gil thought about the prospect. His parents weren't so bad; he actually really liked them. Talking with Clemmie had convinced him that he really didn't share enough.

'Any particular reason for that request? I've already said yes, but I'd like to hear your thinking.'

'My relationship with my parents has broken down irretrievably. Yours doesn't sound as if it has, and… You should hold them close, Gil. Don't leave it until it's too late.'

He reached out, brushing her cheek with his fingers. 'That's a very fine and generous thought, Clemmie. You're right.'

Gil wondered if maybe Clemmie could be convinced to come with him. He'd love to take her on a tour of Australia and have her meet his family. Renew a few ties himself while he was there. That was a question for later, though. The last week had tipped his world upside down, but it was still a little early to ask her to fly more than ten thousand miles to meet his parents.

But it was something to look forward to. He reached out, taking her hand and drawing it to his lips. Clemmie shifted from her seat, sitting on his lap.

'Are we good?' He kissed her and she snuggled into his arms. Of course they were good, but he just wanted to hear her say it.

She looked up at him, her face shining in the darkness. 'Yes, we're good. Although it's getting a little chilly out here.'

'Come back to bed, then.'

CHAPTER THIRTEEN

Gil was fast coming to the conclusion that there was nothing he wouldn't do for Clemmie. Their relationship had been a helter-skelter ride, where missed opportunities, anger and guilt had all done their best to break them apart. But somehow they'd stayed together. Growing and moving forward, leaving the past behind.

Gil felt that he could finally look to the future now. Clemmie remembered so much more than he did, and she'd been three steps ahead of him in this relationship, but she'd waited for him to catch up with her. Now he was ready to take her hand and run towards the future.

'Would you like to go for a bike ride tomorrow? Explore Richmond Park a bit.'

He asked the question as casually as he could. They didn't usually plan their weekends, taking everything as it came, but a little structure wasn't a bad thing.

'I'd have to perch on your handlebars.' She

was packing her briefcase, ready to leave work for the evening, and she looked up, grinning at him.

'The bike shop I go to does hires.'

'I'm not going to go whizzing around Richmond Park, dressed in Lycra. I don't think my legs are up to that.'

'I don't know about that. You have wonderful calves.' She raised her eyebrows and Gil smiled. 'But I was thinking more of a nice Saturday morning ride, to enjoy the scenery.'

'All right. As long as you don't go too fast.'

'I'll stay behind you all the way.'

Clemmie snorted with laughter. 'You will not. Half the pleasure is a nicely shaped rear in front of me to keep my sights on.'

'So sad. You make me feel as if you only want me for my body.' Gil opened his office door before she could reply and Clemmie poked her tongue out at him.

He locked the door behind them, wishing Maggie a good weekend as he walked through Reception. Clemmie went to get her things from her locker, and Gil waited for her outside. The fact that they often left the unit together hadn't excited any particular comment because their work was so closely connected and Gil's way home was in the same general direction as the station, but it was as well not to be too obvious.

'We could follow that path...' Gil pointed across the road to the cycle track that ran around the perimeter of the park. 'Then cut through the woods. I'll be keeping my nicely shaped rear within your line of sight at all times.'

'I'm looking forward to that.'

'If you like it, I'll buy you a bike for Christmas.' The conclusion that he'd been working towards sent a little tingle of pleasure down Gil's spine.

'For Christmas?' She looked up at him, her cheeks reddening slightly.

'Only you'd probably have to keep it at my place. Unless you have cycle lanes where you live.'

'No, there are none close by. And I live on a pretty busy road, so I'm not sure about cycling there.' Clemmie linked her arm with his. 'Probably best to keep it here.'

Christmas seemed a long way away at the moment. But they'd just made a plan, which took it for granted that they'd still be together then. *And* they were walking past the main entrance of the hospital, arm in arm.

'Are we going too fast?' Clemmie removed her hand from the crook of his arm suddenly.

'I'm comfortable with this speed.'

'Me too. Only it's probably best not to make any overt expressions of affection in front of the hospital. Not until I leave next week.'

'So sweeping you off your feet and kissing you is out of the question, then?' Gil liked the way her cheeks became a little pinker when he teased her.

'Absolutely. None of that until we're officially not working together any more.'

'Agreed. Reluctantly, because I very much want to kiss you at the moment.' It felt as if they'd taken another important step, and Gil wanted to mark the moment somehow. The first time they'd talked about the future, knowing that the past had loosened its grip on them. When they got back to his place, he'd make up for lost kissing time.

Clemmie had fussed a little over what to wear, and Gil assured her that jeans and trainers were absolutely fine for the kind of bike ride they were going on, and that they'd be hardly working up a sweat. He walked down to the bike shop the next morning and she was waiting for him as he wheeled the hired bicycle up the front path.

'Ooh. It's a nice one. Not too racy.'

'It'll go at a good speed, and it has gears.' It

was a sturdy bike, without being too heavy, and if Clemmie liked it he'd get her one like this.

'I don't know how to use gears.'

'Don't worry about them for the moment. I'll show you how when we get to a hill.' He reached into the bag that hung from the handle-bars. 'Here's the most important thing.'

Clemmie nodded. 'A helmet. And it matches the bike, as well. Mint green.'

'Yeah, don't be put off by the colour. It's a good helmet that will protect you if you fall off.' And she looked very cute in mint green, her dark hair giving a lift to the colour.

Clemmie tried the helmet on, and Gil checked that it fitted correctly, adjusting the strap carefully under her chin. That wasn't to-tally necessary from a safety point of view, she was perfectly capable of doing it herself, but Gil just liked doing things for Clemmie.

'We're going now? I'm ready.' Clemmie stepped astride the bike, trying out the brakes.

'Yep, if you like. I'll just go and fetch mine.'

Clemmie's fitness might come from constant activity rather than gym work, but she had stamina and strength. Gil already knew that. He'd tested every part of her body, measur-ing its balance and power against his. She rode ahead of him for a while, setting a very respect-able pace.

They stopped for a while, when the path wound upwards into the woods, and he showed her how to use the gears. After a few hiccups, she got the hang of it, and they rode to the top of the hill and then turned to make their way back down.

'I really like this. It's not as much work as it looks.' She rode beside him on the wide path, careful to leave plenty of space for pedestri-ans, and an overtaking lane for other cyclists. 'Oops!'

She wobbled, almost coming off the bike as three sports bikes shot past her down the hill. Gil instinctively stretched out his hand, but she regained her balance. But the other cy-clists were going too fast, and as they hit a bump in the path further down, one of them swerved violently.

'Go...' Clemmie obviously wasn't confident about going any faster down the hill, but she urged Gil on. She could see the same as he had—the guy had been going at such speed that he'd practically flown off the bike, land-ing a good six feet away at the side of the path.

He got to the man before his companions had a chance to turn around and pedal back up the hill. But before he could stop him, the guy had got to his feet.

'Hey. Are you all right?' Gil would have preferred he'd stayed down a little longer, so that he could check him out before he started to move around.

'Yeah, I think so…' The man grinned, squaring his shoulders, and then doubled up with pain. 'Agh!'

'I'm a doctor. Sit down for a moment and let me take a look at you.'

'Uh… Yeah, thanks.'

Gil walked the man slowly over to a nearby bench and sat him down. His first instinct was to check on his head, but he could see that the guy's cycle helmet was undamaged and that was a good sign. All the same, he carefully unbuckled it, taking it off.

'Did you hit your head?'

'Don't think so. Came down on my shoulder. Bloody stupid… Going far too fast.'

Gil was inclined to agree with him, but that wasn't his first concern at the moment. He felt someone jostle him from behind, trying to move him out of the way, and then heard Clemmie's sharp rebuke.

'Give him some room, please. My friend and I are both doctors.'

'What kind of doctor?' There was a hint of cockiness in the male voice that replied.

'The kind you're always pleased to have around when someone falls off their bike.' The crispness in Clemmie's tone brooked no argument, and Gil smiled, imagining that her expression was just as fierce.

'Give it a rest, Brad.' His patient tried to move but his face creased in pain.

'You too. Stay still, please.' Clemmie sat down on the bench beside him. 'I'm Clemmie, by the way.'

'Nathan. I'd shake your hand but…'

'You'd have to move to do it. So we'll give that a miss, shall we?'

Clemmie had already fetched the first-aid kit from Gil's bike, and was unzipping the bag. She handed him the penlight and Gil checked that Nathan's pupils reacted correctly to the light. He could feel no bumps on Nathan's head, and he seemed to have no other symptoms of concussion.

'Looks like it's just his shoulder,' Clemmie murmured, gently moving Gil on to the next thing on his to-do list. He nodded, glad of her prompt. His own experience meant that he was always very careful about the possibility of anyone bumping their head, and Clemmie was watching over him, carefully guiding him.

They removed Nathan's cycling top, and even the most cursory examination would have been enough to reveal that he'd broken his collarbone, and probably one of the small bones in his wrist, as well. Clemmie unfolded two triangular bandages from the first-aid kit, helping Gil to immobilise Nathan's arm.

'Thanks. That feels much better now.' Nathan seemed about to try to stand, and Clemmie stopped him.

'We'll need you to come down to the hospital, for an X-ray. It looks as if you've broken your collarbone, and possibly your wrist.'

'Really? It doesn't feel too bad.' Nathan tried to sit up a little straighter and grunted in pain. 'You might be right…'

Now it was just a matter of getting him there. Calling for an ambulance seemed to be the only way, but the crew might have to walk to get to them, as it was unlikely that the ambulance could navigate the narrower parts of the track. Then Clemmie nudged Gil, pointing down towards the bottom of the hill. An off-road parks department vehicle had drawn up, and a couple of men were surveying a felled tree.

'That'll do, won't it?'

It would. Gil sent one of Nathan's riding companions down to talk to the men, and within ten minutes they were helping Nathan into the vehicle and their bikes were being loaded onto the back. The driver manoeuvred slowly and carefully down the hill, taking them round to the park entrance that stood opposite the hospital, and then driving them across to the entrance of A & E. There were a few raised eyebrows from the ambulance crews who were waiting there, but as soon as they saw Nathan, they set about helping him from the back seat and into a wheelchair.

'Thanks, guys.' Nathan gave them a smile as a nurse wheeled him away to be examined. 'Sorry to spoil your Saturday.'

'No problem. Take care...' Clemmie gave him a wave and turned away to retrieve their bikes, which had been propped up against the wall by the entrance.

Gil finally allowed himself a frustrated grimace. 'I take a girl out and what happens? Someone comes flying off their bike and we end up back at work.'

'Stop it.' Clemmie bumped her shoulder against his arm. 'What were you going to do, ride past and leave him there?'

'No, I suppose not.' Gil had wanted today to be perfect, though. The first day when their future seemed clear.

'Don't be so grumpy, then. Tell you what—

why don't we walk over and I can show Jahira this bike?'

'She'll only want to try and ride it. One person falling off a bike is about as much as I can take in a day.'

'We'll just let her put the helmet on and sit on the saddle. You can hold the bike steady and she won't be going anywhere. You asked her mum whether it was okay to encourage Jahira to take an interest in cycling again, didn't you?'

'Yes, I did. Jahira's been asking her about getting a new bike, and her mum thinks it's a good idea as long as she keeps to cycle lanes in future. I'm sure she wouldn't object.'

'Well, then. We can take some photos for Jahira's memory book. There are plenty of pages to spare for the new memories she's making.' Clemmie reached for her cycle helmet, putting it onto her head. 'And I want to show off the cycle helmet, as well. I like the colour.'

Gil made a mental note that the bike he bought Clemmie—and the cycle helmet— would both be mint green. 'Okay, then. And then we'll go and get some lunch?'

'Sounds good to me.'

Suddenly the day *was* perfect. Because Clemmie was smiling.

* * *

Gil had been keeping things from her. On her last afternoon at Barney's they'd been working in his office and he'd received a call. He'd got to his feet, hurrying out of the room, and she'd followed him, wondering what was up. When he'd got to the patients' sitting room there had been a loud chorus of *'Surprise!'* and then party poppers, a cake and alcohol-free punch.

Everyone had traded kisses with her, apart from Gil. His would come later.

'I talked to my boss on the phone this morning.' Clemmie followed him into his house, putting her flowers down carefully in the hall. 'He's really interested in some of the things we've been doing in the last six weeks and wants me to write a full report. Compare and contrast the two units.'

Gil nodded. 'Sounds great. I'd be interested in seeing that. There'll be something I can learn from it, no doubt.'

'No doubt.' Clemmie liked the way that he always looked outwards, not locked into his own way of doing things. It was a professional and personal breath of fresh air.

He wrapped his arms around her shoulders, kissing her. 'I guess that means I won't be seeing so much of you next week…'

Clemmie turned her lips down in an expression of regret. 'Probably not. He's talking about a presentation at a meeting that's taking place the week after next, so I'll have to get it done next week. It'll probably mean a few late nights at work. I'll miss you—'

Gil put his finger across her lips. 'This is important. And just think—I'll be missing you more than I can say, so…' He whispered in her ear, telling her all the ways he might show her just how much he'd been missing her, when next weekend finally came around.

'That sounds wonderful.' This was more difficult than Clemmie had thought it would be. She trusted Gil and knew that history wasn't going to repeat itself. All the same, their fond goodbye at the end of the conference and everything that had happened subsequently were hard to banish from her thoughts.

'And just to make sure that you know where to find me.' He took her hand, leading her into the sitting room. An envelope was propped up on the mantelpiece and he handed it to her.

'What's this?' Clemmie opened the envelope and then started to laugh. There was a small card inside, with Gil's mobile number written on it. Along with his email address, his landline number and his direct line at work. Gil knew how she felt, and he was making this parting different from the last.

'Just to give you a few options.' He was smiling broadly.

'Thank you. I'll keep it safe.' Clemmie fetched her handbag from the hallway, taking out her purse and slipping the card into one of the pockets behind her credit cards. 'Would you like my numbers at home?'

'Yes, and your email address. I'll be calling you, and if you don't answer, I'll be turning up in person to find you.'

'With a glass slipper in your hand?'

'Yeah. Or a cycle helmet.' He kissed her and Clemmie flung her arms around his neck. This time, things were going to be different.

CHAPTER FOURTEEN

GIL HAD CALLED every evening, at nine o'clock on the dot. They'd talked about everything: the finer points of her presentation and what their days had brought. Gil had reported that the romance between Edward and Caroline was very definitely on, and that Jahira sent her love. The best part was right before they said goodbye, when he told her how much he missed her and that he'd call her again tomorrow. The warmth in his voice was always the same, always something that Clemmie could depend on.

She'd emailed the text of her presentation through to him every evening, and at lunchtime the following day there was always an email from Gil, answering questions and giving his own opinions on what she'd written. Clemmie arrived home at eight o'clock on Friday and decided she couldn't wait a whole hour to speak to him.

'What are you doing?'

Gil seemed a little out of breath when he answered. 'Digging.'

'Ah. Frustrating day?'

'It's been interesting. We had a new patient in and he's very angry. Very frustrated. He took a swing at Elaine at one point, but fortunately she managed to duck. Anya talked him down and I spent some time with his wife this afternoon, discussing how we can all help him. The situation's under control and he was much calmer when I left him just now.'

'That's good. Poor Elaine. I'm sure she doesn't need something like that.' The young nurse had become more confident in her role since Jeannie's fall in the greenhouse, and Clemmie hoped that this incident hadn't undone any of the work that Gil had done in reassuring her.

'I had a chat with her, and she knows it's nothing personal. She has all the makings of a very good nurse. How's your day been?'

Clemmie grinned. 'Productive. I've finished my presentation and my boss has given it the thumbs-up. Two thumbs, actually, and a *"Very well done, Clemmie."* Which was amazing because he's generally a man of few words.'

She heard Gil laugh. 'Of course he did. I think it's an exceptional piece of work.'

'Thank you. I couldn't have done it without you.' In so many ways. Gil hadn't just given her the experience of running a unit that she needed; he'd been there for Clemmie. Giving her the confidence to break new ground in her presentation, rather than simply report on her findings.

'You did it all by yourself. I just watched and marvelled. So you're free tomorrow, then?'

'Yes. Do you want me to come down to Richmond so that you're on hand if you need to pop into the unit to see your new patient? I have a furniture delivery coming first thing, but I'll be able to make it to you by lunchtime.'

'Or I could come to you. I've spoken with the doctor who'll be on duty tomorrow and he's perfectly capable of handling the situation. One of the things you learn when you're running your own unit: how to have confidence in your staff, and realise that the place isn't going to fall to pieces if you take some time off.'

'One of the things I'm going to learn? Or one of the things you learned?'

'All right. One of the things I learned. So how about it? I can come to you first thing tomorrow, or you can come down here if you prefer.'

Clemmie wanted Gil to come to her flat, but she supposed she should let him know what he might be in for. 'I could offer you a fabulous lunch and something glamorous to do in the afternoon, but you may find yourself putting some furniture together...'

'Where's your sense of adventure? Putting furniture together can be glamorous, too.'

'Well, I'm pretty excited. I've been sleeping on an old futon that someone gave me for the last six months, and now that my bedroom's painted and I've got some nice furniture, it'll be much more comfortable.'

'In that case, I insist on coming to you. You might need some help with the bed.'

Clemmie laughed. 'I definitely will. And by the way, you're to stop digging immediately, Gil. I don't want you working all of your frustration off on a patch of ground.'

He chuckled. 'There's only one cure for that kind of frustration, sweetheart, and digging isn't going to do it...'

The delivery van arrived at eight the following morning, and Gil's car drew up behind it while the men were stacking boxes in Clemmie's hall. He helped them in with the final few and gave them a cheery wave as they left. The door slammed behind him, and Clemmie found herself in his arms.

'I don't suppose you missed me, did you?' He grinned down at her.

'I missed you.' But now the past had been overwritten. That felt special.

'Mm. How much?' He crowded her back against the plastic-wrapped mattress that was propped up against the wall.

'Seriously.' She smiled up at him. 'You want to try it out already?'

'This is probably the last time it'll be at quite this angle...' He ran his hands from her shoulders to her wrists, and then pinioned her arms above her head.

Tempting. *Very* tempting. 'Far be it from me to add a note of practicality, but...what happens when things get a little bit too passionate and it falls on top of us?'

'I get to rescue you. And you get to be *very* grateful?' Gil gave her that playful grin that made Clemmie go weak at the knees.

She stood on her toes, planting a kiss onto his lips. As Gil moved closer, the pressure of his body against hers and the subtle give of the mattress against her back *were* enticing. All she needed to do was let Gil support her weight...

'You're right. It's not going to stay upright for much longer.' He stepped away from her.

'Tease! I was just starting to like the idea.'

His lips curved. Gil clearly was, too.

'I dare say we can prop it a bit more securely against the wall in the bedroom.' Clemmie opened the bedroom door, surveying the empty room.

'Sounds like a very sensible plan.' Gil kissed her. 'Are you sure I can wait that long?'

'Positive. Because you know I'll deliver…'

They'd unpacked the chest of drawers and Gil had helped her manoeuvre it into the bedroom, along with the boxes that contained the wardrobe. The bed had come next and had taken an hour to put together. Trying the mattress out, first vertically and then horizontally, had taken rather longer, but Clemmie had found it an enormously satisfying experience, and there was no doubt that Gil agreed with her.

It was so good having him here. Cooking together, and puzzling over the leaflet that gave instructions on how to put the wardrobe together. Clemmie loaded up the wardrobe and Gil took apart the steel-framed clothes racks that she'd been using, stacking them neatly with the flattened boxes in the hallway.

Waking up with him was even better. Feeling his warm body curled around hers, in a comfortable bed. Sunshine filtering through the window, and everything neat and tidy, her clothes folded in the chest of drawers and hanging in the wardrobe.

Gil made her breakfast in bed, and then insisted they finish the job. His car was bigger than hers, and the old futon and all the rubbish in the hallway could be crammed into the back, so that they could take it for disposal.

'Lunch?' He grinned at her as they drove out of the recycling centre. 'Or would you prefer me to cook while you stare at your new bedroom?'

'I'm taking you to lunch. Thank you so much for helping, Gil.'

'My pleasure. Thank you for making me a part of your milestone.'

It felt like a milestone. She'd finally got herself on her feet, enough to furnish and decorate one room in her flat, at least. The others would follow. Everything else would follow.

Clemmie directed him to her favourite local pub, and they ordered their meal. She tipped her glass against his.

'I feel as if I'm finally getting my life back together again. I have my own flat and some furniture. And there's no more feeling as if I'm being held hostage while Harry tries to throw spanners in the works with the divorce.'

He took a sip of his drink. 'Two years must have seemed like a long time to wait, in those circumstances.'

'Five.' It had been a long time, but it was over now. 'A divorce only takes two years if

both parties agree in writing. Harry refused
to do that.'

'Five years? And you were married for eighteen months…' Clemmie heard the sudden
tension in his tone and her heart sank. Stupid. She'd been basking in the pleasure of the
weekend and let her guard down.

'Um…closer to a year.'

'You said it was eighteen months.'

Why did Gil have to remember everything
she said? Or was it just all the things she didn't
want him to remember?

'Yes. It was eighteen months, then.'

'You said that you needed an anchor when
you married him. Do you mind telling me
why?' He was obviously trying to keep this
casual, but there was a hint of tension behind
the questions.

'It was a lot of things, Gil. Can't we talk
about something else?'

He nodded. 'Yeah. Sure.'

Saying it was easy. Gil was smiling and talk-
ative again, but Clemmie could still see a cloud
of doubt in his eyes. It was so easy to overlook
Gil's vulnerability because he seemed so very
strong.

And there was nothing wrong with his maths.
Five years plus eighteen months was six and a

half years. Leaving only six months for a broken heart and a rushed engagement.

He was quiet on the way back home, and as they walked back from his car, he put his arm around her shoulders, as if he wanted to protect her from harm. That he couldn't do, but after all they'd been to each other—all they *were* to each other—maybe they were strong enough for this. She let them into the flat, walking through into the sitting room.

'Okay. I'll tell you…'

Gil didn't want to know. All of his instincts were telling him that he should stop her now, and they could go on with their weekend. Go on with their lives. But Clemmie had kept this secret from him for a reason. It might well break them apart if she told him, but he'd never be able to touch her again if he knew that he'd done something that hurt her so much she couldn't speak about it. At least this way, they had a chance.

Gil sat down. He thought he knew what she was about to say, but he didn't dare believe it.

'One thing, Clemmie. If you're going to tell me, please don't leave anything out.'

She nodded, coming to sit beside him. Gil took her hand and gave it a squeeze, in the hope of communicating a reassurance that he didn't feel.

'I shouldn't have let you guess.'

That could mean one of two things. Either she shouldn't have kept this secret, or she should have kept it better. Gil decided not to ask.

'What's done is done. Tell me now.'

Her mouth twisted. 'We had something special, you know that. It all happened so fast, but it seemed so right, from the very start. You heard me and you saw me. You told me that you loved me, and we exchanged numbers because we were going to…' A tear ran down her cheek.

Her words hit him like a hammer blow. 'You mean…we made plans.'

Clemmie nodded. 'Yes, we did. You said that you loved your work but you felt it consumed you sometimes, and that I'd made you see that there were other things in life. I thought that this would be a new start for both of us, and when you didn't answer my calls I…' Her voice dropped to a whisper. 'I thought you'd ghosted me, Gil. And that it was a cruel thing to have done.'

'I made promises and…then I broke them. You were right to think me cruel.'

Clemmie frowned. 'You're nothing of the sort. You were in hospital with a brain injury—

how on earth could you be expected to answer your phone?'

Gil's head sank into his hands, in despair. She had to know…

'When I was recovering, I managed to get my phone charged and I deleted all the calls and messages that were on it. I couldn't accept what was going on in my life and I just withdrew. I didn't want to speak to anyone.'

Clemmie reddened suddenly, staring at him. Maybe she was putting two and two together and realising that he *was* responsible for all the hurt she'd felt.

'I don't blame you for that. It was a perfectly natural reaction to what had happened to you.'

'It was *me* that did it, not the TBI. You married Harry because I broke your heart, didn't you?'

She pressed her lips together. 'I needed someone who was present, and who wouldn't leave me. That was everything to do with where I was in my life back then, and nothing to do with you. I gave up on you too soon, because I was ready to believe that no one could care about me the way you seemed to.'

'Don't…' Gil felt tears prick at the sides of his eyes. 'Never believe it was your fault, because it wasn't.'

His TBI had been the turning point that

had forced him to slow down and strike a better work-life balance, but deep down Gil had known that he needed to do that before then. What if Clemmie had sensed it, too? What if she'd given up on him because she'd known in her heart he would never change? All she was guilty of was a willingness to see the best in him.

But the worst was still there. He'd found a healthier balance, a better way to live his life, but he was still the same man. Still determined to succeed in whatever he did, which was really just another way of saying that he was driven.

He had no doubt that he'd told the truth when he'd said he loved Clemmie. He loved her now. Maybe that was the best reason of all to let her go.

'Can't you say something, Gil…?' Clemmie was looking at him imploringly. Despite everything, she still trusted him.

'I'm sorry.' How could he tell her that the only thing he could do to make things better was to leave, when it was the last thing in the world he wanted to do?

'I know this is hard and…' She shrugged. 'We both should have known that a completely new start wasn't going to be possible. And I'd understand it if you felt that you don't remember what happened between us because I'd put you under stress—'

'No. I won't hear you say that, Clemmie. You had no part in what happened to me. You make me happy now, and even if I can't remember it, I know you made me happy then.'

'Then *be* happy, Gil.' Frustration sounded in her voice.

He shook his head. 'That's not enough. If I can't know that I'll keep my promises, how can our relationship ever be a safe place for both of us?'

'It *is* our safe place. Don't take that away from me. I don't deserve it.' Her cheeks flushed a deeper red with anger, and suddenly Gil knew. This time wouldn't be the same as the last, because Clemmie knew that she deserved better and was strong enough to go out and take it.

'I'm sorry. I can't see a way forward and… I won't hurt you again.'

'What if I don't let you? What if I tell you that I'll stick with you and that we can get through this?' The way that Clemmie's eyes flashed, so defiantly, almost made Gil weaken.

'You'd have stuck with me when I had my TBI as well, wouldn't you?'

She didn't even have to think about it. 'Of course I would. What's wrong with that?'

Nothing. And everything. Gil had just realised how much Clemmie had forgiven him for, without even asking for an explanation. The woman in the picture hadn't deserved to share the bad days after his TBI, and Clemmie didn't deserve to risk her future with someone who had already hurt her so badly.

'You kept this from me, Clemmie. Because you knew it would change everything.'

She hesitated. In that moment, Gil knew he was right. 'I thought you'd be…that you'd feel responsible.'

'I *am* responsible. What I did then, the little things that added up to all that rejection and hurt, was less to do with my TBI and a lot more to do with the person I was. You've changed, but I'm still the same as I always have been. I can't promise to be the man that makes you happy and I won't settle for anything less.'

He'd said it now. There was no point in staying any longer, when he wasn't going to change his mind. Gil got to his feet, aware that Clemmie was staring at him. But when he walked away from her, she didn't stop him.

As he walked out into the sunlight, it seemed to sear into his brain, and the old sensation that he was about to lose his balance almost stopped him in his tracks. He had the strangest feeling that the world was unfamiliar, as if it had changed somehow when he wasn't looking.

Gil got into his car. This he could handle—he knew exactly how to deal with disorientation. Emotion and loss were less easily put aside, but if they allowed Clemmie to get on with her life and be happy, he'd take them.

He sat for a moment, breathing steadily and mentally checking that he was okay to drive. The world began to resolve itself into sharp focus again, but it was suddenly a harsher and colder place. Gil started the ignition and pulled away from the kerb.

As soon as she heard the front door close, Clemmie sprang to her feet, running to the window. Gil didn't look back. When he got into his car he sat for a moment, seemingly deep in thought, and one last thread of agonising hope held her motionless. Then it snapped as Gil started the engine and drove away.

This time she'd survive. Not because she loved Gil any less, but because she knew she had the strength to carry on. And because she had no regrets.

She'd taken the risk of loving him and she'd done it with her eyes wide open. Knowing what she did now, she would still have taken that risk, because her relationship with Gil had brought her closure. She'd loved him almost from the moment she'd met him, and now she knew that she hadn't made a mistake, in loving him then or in loving him now. Nothing could take that from her.

If Gil could only trust himself. If he could just believe in himself the way she believed in him. Clemmie knew that Gil loved her, and that he was only doing what he thought was right. That was the most heartbreaking part of it all.

She walked into the kitchen, opening the door of the fridge. There was a bottle of wine, and there was ice cream, too. But it was far too early in the day for either of those remedies, and she wasn't going to crumble the way she had before. This time it was going to be different.

CHAPTER FIFTEEN

'ARE YOU READY, Jahira?' Gil stopped in the open doorway of her room.

'No. Are you?'

Jahira could be a lot wiser than her years suggested at times. Gil laughed. 'No. I dare say I'll manage, though.'

'Me too.'

Gil had been intending to give Jahira a final barrage of encouragement before she left rehab today, but he reckoned that those few words pretty much summed it up. No one knew what the future would hold, but Jahira was ready for it, and that was all anyone could ask.

'You know where I am, don't you? Don't be a stranger.'

'I'll come back and check up on you.' Jahira grinned at him.

She'd caught Gil staring silently out at the garden yesterday and asked him what the matter was. Two weeks, and he still couldn't think about Clemmie without someone noticing the pain on his face. The only solution was not to think about her at all when anyone was around, but that was difficult when there was so much here to remind him of her.

'You do that. And don't forget, if you have any questions or difficulties…' Gil shrugged. 'It says all that in your discharge leaflet. Just put my number in your phone and use it, eh? Or I'll start to feel that you've forgotten me.'

Jahira gave a dry chuckle, picking up the phone that lay next to her chair. 'Can't have that, can we, Doctor? What's your number, then?'

Gil took his phone from his pocket and handed it to her. 'This is the number you can get me on twenty-four-seven. I want to hear about how you're doing when you go back to college.'

'That might be a long story…'

'I'll get myself a cup of tea.'

Jahira nodded, flipping his phone against hers. A beep announced that the two phones had linked up and exchanged numbers. It was efficient, but it didn't compare with the photograph that Gil still carried in his wallet.

'I forgot to show you this.' Jahira handed him an envelope, and he saw Clemmie's writing on it. Gil hadn't lost the feeling that Clemmie was close by, watching over him, and these small reminders of her always brought both pleasure and pain.

'What's this?'

'See for yourself.'

He flipped open the envelope, taking out the card that was inside. 'Puppies. Nice.'

'Cute. Puppies are cute.'

'All right. Cute puppies.' Gil grinned as he opened the card. He expected that Clemmie had thought they were cute, too.

Inside, a gift card for a chain of bookstores, and a message from Clemmie.

A little something to help you with your studies. The world's out there, waiting for you to take it by storm!

'Do you think Clemmie would mind if I called her? To say thank you.' Jahira's words dragged Gil back from the gaping hole of longing that was threatening to swallow him up.

'No, I think she'd love to hear from you. You can give her the full story of exactly how you're planning to take the world by storm. You have her number?' Gil congratulated himself on managing to get the words out without choking.

'Yeah. She gave it to me when she left.'

Gil decided on a change of subject. 'What time are your parents coming to fetch you?'

'They phoned just now, so they'll be half an hour.' Jahira rose from her seat, grabbing the walker that stood beside it. 'I've gotta say good-bye to everyone.'

'I'm doing my morning walkabout. You're going my way?' Jahira's bright independence was one thing. But Gil knew that today was going to be an emotional one for her, and she might like a little company.

Jahira grinned. 'Depends which way you're going, doesn't it, Doc?'

Jahira was a little teary by the time her parents arrived, but a hug from her mother and father made her smile again. Then Sarah flung her arms around Jahira's neck and the two girls started to talk excitedly, while Jahira's mother packed the last of her things into her bag.

'I hear someone's going home…' A familiar voice sounded behind him, and Gil turned to see Sam standing there, holding a bunch of flowers.

'Where did you hear that? You've got this place bugged?'

'Never you mind.' Sam tapped the side of her nose. 'I have my sources.'

Sam delivered the flowers into Jahira's lap, and the teenager smiled shyly, obviously only half remembering Sam's name. Her father stepped in, reminding Jahira that Sam was the surgeon who had operated on her, and shaking Sam's hand until her arm looked in danger of falling off.

'Haven't you forgotten something?' Gil smiled at her.

'No. Don't think so...' Sam looked around and then the penny dropped. 'Oh, you mean the twins. They're in Reception with Maggie. She's masterminding the cuddle rota. Yanis is keeping an eye out to make sure we don't lose one of them.'

'That's only going to get more difficult when they start walking.' Gil grinned.

'Don't, Gil. We're working on an event horizon of about five minutes at the moment. Anything beyond that, we'll take as it comes.'

And the next five minutes held a whole world of goodness for Sam. Her face was glowing with the kind of happiness that lived in each moment, always there and always sustaining her. Just thinking about it allowed Gil to breathe, as if some of it had rubbed off on him.

'I'm going to do the walk?' Jahira tugged at his sleeve.

Gil nodded. 'You'd better. You deserve it.'

'What's the walk?' Sarah asked.

'You'll see.' Jahira took her arm, ready to go. General practice at the hospital was to discharge anyone who had difficulty walking in a wheelchair. But Jahira was steady enough on her feet now and 'the walk' was more important. Her father picked up her bag and the flowers, leaving Sarah and her mother to walk on either side of her.

'I love this part…' Sam whispered, falling into step beside Gil, who was following Jahira, ready to step forward and steady her if she lost her balance.

So did he. He'd insisted on walking out of the rehab unit himself, seven years ago, and Gil knew just how it felt. And now there was a little more ceremony to it. Many of the staff and some of the patients had gathered in Reception, along with Edward and Caroline, who had come back to visit Jahira and stayed to see her off. When Jahira walked through, they all applauded.

Jahira's mother was so intent on saying goodbye and thanking everyone that she left Sarah to take Jahira's arm and lead her out of the main doors. Jahira took a deep breath as she stepped outside. Gil knew that feeling. It didn't matter that he'd spent most of his time in the garden when he was a patient here. That first breath of air that he'd filled his lungs with when he'd left the building with his discharge papers in his pocket had seemed so much fresher.

The two girls sat down on the bench outside the building, while Jahira's father went to fetch the car. Sarah was talking to Jahira, her arm around her shoulders, and Jahira was nodding and smiling.

'They're so adorable together.' Sam smiled. 'Teenage sweethearts...'

Gil chuckled. 'Yeah. I miss that feeling of having everything in front of me, sometimes.'

Sam's elbow found his ribs. 'Don't get soppy on me, Gil. That "everything" that we had in front of us wasn't all plain sailing, for either of us.'

Very true. But the void he was looking at now wasn't all that appealing either.

'We both made it through, though.' Sam had, at least. He was still a work in progress. 'By the way, I'm going to be taking an extended leave soon. I'll be off from next week.'

'That's a bit sudden, isn't it? Are you going anywhere nice?'

He was keeping a promise. Clemmie was still here, still guiding him.

'I'm going back to Australia, to see my folks. I'll be away for six weeks.'

'Six weeks!' Sam's eyebrows shot up. 'You're sure you'll survive that?'

Gil shrugged. 'I'm going to give it a go. I won't be staying with them for the whole time. I thought I'd take the opportunity to just sink my roots into home soil for a while. Jack Llewellyn is going to be taking over the running of the unit while I'm away.' Jack had worked here as a doctor for three years now, and Gil was confident in his ability to keep everything running smoothly.

'I'm sure he'll do a good job. But tell him to call me if he wants to talk anything over.'

'Thanks. I will.' Gil was aware that Sam was staring at him thoughtfully. 'What?'

'It sounds like a great idea. But is everything all right? None of your family are ill, are they?'

'No, everyone's fine. It's just time I went, that's all.'

Gil leaned back in his seat on the veranda. His parents' house was situated in the hills around Brisbane, and at dusk the city was just a few pinpricks of light in the distance. The jacaranda trees were in flower, shedding carpets of iridescent purple blooms, and a huge mulberry tree in the back yard was in full fruit. Gil had spent the afternoon helping gather the mulberries, climbing up into the spreading branches and shaking them so that the ripe fruit fell onto a tarpaulin, spread across the ground.

His mother walked towards him, pulling on a thin cardigan and sitting down.

'Aren't you cold?'

Gil shook his head. 'Nah. If we were in London, I'd be doing laps around the veranda to keep warm at this time of year.'

His mother chuckled. 'Turned you into a tough guy, has it?'

Yes and no. Gil felt more vulnerable now than he'd ever done, as if there were an open wound around his heart that only Clemmie could heal.

'You should come for a visit. See for yourself.'

'The Tower of London in the snow?' Gil's Christmas card last year had obviously registered in his mother's mind. 'I'd like to see that.'

'You'd have to pick your time if you want snow. We get a lot less of it than the Christmas cards suggest. You're more likely to encounter cold winds and horizontal rain.'

'Sounds lovely.' His mother turned her mouth down.

'It's different. If you ever have six weeks to spare, I think you'd like exploring London.' The idea of his parents *ever* having six weeks to spare to do anything just for pleasure was a little alien to Gil. Although his mother didn't seem so tightly strung as he remembered her.

'You'd be surprised, Gil. I might just persuade your father to take you up on that and we'll turn up on your doorstep, expecting you to show us around.'

'Nothing would give me greater pleasure.' Maybe Gil hadn't said that enough. He probably hadn't said it at all, reckoning that the idea would be instantly deemed impossible.

His mother stared out at the darkening horizon for a moment. 'You want to fix a date?'

'Yes. Be warned that if we do, then I'll hold you to it.'

'I guess I deserve that.' His mother's face suddenly seemed lined with regret. 'You know… I should have had more time for you and your sisters. When you were growing up.'

Gil shrugged. 'I never felt that. You were building your career. Doing things that mattered.'

'When did you stop saying what was on your mind, Gil? I'm quite aware of my own mistakes.'

'None of us is perfect. You always loved me and I love you back.'

His mother nodded, obviously pleased with the sentiment. 'I've realised a few awkward truths in the last few years, Gil. When the doctor told me that my liver wasn't in good shape and I had to stop drinking, it was a wake-up call…'

'What? You never said anything to me about your liver, Mum.'

'Stopping drinking did the trick.' Gil's mother waved his concern away. 'I'll show you the scans if you don't believe me. I dare say you'll understand what they mean a lot better than I do. And you're a fine one to talk. How long was it before you admitted to having been laid up with a traumatic brain injury?'

Gil stretched his fingers, staring at the two that obstinately refused to straighten as much as the others. 'I didn't want to worry you.'

His mother snorted her disdain. 'Stop it, Gil. You know that's an excuse as well as I do, don't you?'

'Yes, I do. And I'm going to make a change, Mum. Next time something happens I'll be calling you.'

'You'd better. I know how that all works, Gil. You were always the one that was most like me. Even when you were a toddler, I'd put something in your way and you'd just climb over it, however high it was. I encouraged you in that. In my eyes it made you strong…' His mother shrugged, staring out at the sunset.

'Stop beating yourself up, Mum. You gave me a great childhood and the determination I needed to face obstacles, and to change when I needed to. There's nothing wrong with that.'

'I'm glad you see it that way. And I'm glad you found a way to change sooner than I did.' His mother shot him an amused look. 'I still can't get my head around you in a garden. Having the patience to grow apple trees.'

'It helps that London has a bit more rain than you do here.' Gil shrugged. 'I'm not sure how much I've really changed, though. You said it yourself. I always had a driven streak.'

'Yes, you did. It's what you do with it that matters, though. I knew you'd changed pace, and that you'd made that work for you. I remembered that when I was told that I needed to lay off the booze if I was going to make old bones, because I knew I'd have to find another way to wind down and get a night's sleep.'

'And the yoga's working?'

His mother nodded. 'Much as the gardening is. I've come to love it.'

Gil sighed. He should have had this conversation a long time ago. 'I've been away too long, haven't I? I've missed all this, and I've missed you, too.'

'You're here now. I'm interested to know why exactly…' His mother leaned towards him, a querulous tone to her voice. 'Come on. I might have brought you up to deny your own weaknesses, but I'm officially changing my tune now. Let's see if you're the man I think you are...'

Gil laughed. His mother could never resist throwing down a challenge and he couldn't resist picking it up. Maybe she was right and it was what you did with that instinct that mattered.

'There was someone... Her name's Clemmie.'

'Nice name. She made you happy?'

More than he'd ever been. More than he ever would be again. 'Yes. Very happy.'

'I'm starting to like her a lot. Did you pull your socks up and make *her* happy?'

Gil chuckled. 'Yep. I pulled my socks up. It's complicated.'

His mother folded her hands in her lap. 'I'm retired, kiddo. I've got all the time in the world for complicated.'

Gil considered the prospect. He'd come all this way because he'd promised Clemmie he would, and she'd been right. If he really wanted to know what kind of man he was, this wasn't a bad place to start.

'I met Clemmie before I had my brain injury. I didn't mean to, but I hurt her very badly. She gave me a second chance, though...'

'That's good, isn't it?'

'Clemmie's a good person. She has a capacity for seeing the best in everyone.'

His mother nodded. 'You mean you think you're not good enough for her?'

Gil shrugged. That went without saying. 'I was proud, and I wanted to be the best in whatever I did. I wouldn't acknowledge my weaknesses to myself, let alone anyone else. That's what hurt her so much the first time, and I'm not sure I'm so very different now.'

His mother reached across, squeezing his hand. Gil wouldn't have dreamed of having this conversation with her a few months ago, but maybe this was why Clemmie had told him to come here if he ever reached a crossroads in his life.

'You and me both. And yet look at us. Sitting here with a sunset, talking about it.'

Gil chuckled. 'It's not that easy, though, is it?'

'Forget easy. It's a matter of reassessing your goals and choosing a bit more carefully this time. Was it easy for you, coming here?'

No. It had been a leap of faith. Wanting his relationship with his parents to be different and trusting in Clemmie's judgement.

'Let's just say that this visit was well overdue.'

'Don't sugar-coat it, Gil—a *no* will do. But

I'm grateful that you came. I'd be willing to bet that if you want to be with this girl, then you'll make that work, too. Nothing comes easy, but that's what we both do. We make things work. If she were here, I'd tell her that she can trust you to do that if you set your mind to it.'

Gil didn't reply, and his mother got to her feet, her fingers brushing across his shoulder as she walked behind him, in an expression of tenderness. 'I'm going to get some juice. You want a beer?'

Gil shook his head. 'Actually, I was going to see if I could mix a virgin version of the cappuccino cocktail. One that doesn't just taste like a cold cup of cappuccino.'

His mother gave a dry laugh. 'Yeah, go for it, then. If you can manage that, then you'll manage anything…'

CHAPTER SIXTEEN

CLEMMIE HAD PROMISED herself that today would be the last day she'd have to clean paint spatter out of her hair before she went to bed. The kitchen ceiling was going to be painted by tonight, however many people called her. But now she'd climbed down off the ladder to answer a question from one of the junior doctors at work, which really could have waited until Monday, she might as well make herself a cup of tea.

It had been four weeks. She'd missed Gil every day and every night. She'd cried, and sometimes the weight in her heart seemed so heavy that she could hardly move. But she'd carried on. He'd shown her how to do that.

As she sipped her tea, her phone rang again. Clemmie looked at the caller ID and her sharp intake of breath sent the tea into her windpipe. She grabbed the phone, stabbing at the answer button, and then dropped it back onto the counter as she started to choke.

'Clemmie! Clemmie!' She could hear Gil's voice coming from the phone, but she was still fighting for breath and she couldn't reply. He was calling her name, sounding more and more alarmed, and then the doorbell rang.

Forget visitors, she had more important things to think about right now. Then she heard an urgent knocking on her front door and the sound of Gil's voice outside. He'd been right here, and must have found someone to buzz him into the lobby. Clemmie felt a wash of relief. Now all she had to do was get to the door...

Or not. From the sound of it, Gil had just put his shoulder to the door. Breaking it down didn't seem such a bad idea at the moment. Clemmie put her fist to her stomach, grasping it with the other hand, and bent over the countertop. One sharp shove and the liquid stuck in her windpipe suddenly dislodged.

The door gave. She could breathe now, but she was still wheezing, and Clemmie sank to the floor as Gil appeared in the kitchen doorway.

'Okay...' She held up her hand before he could lift her to her feet to perform more abdominal thrusts. Gil knelt down beside her, one hand rubbing her back and the other supporting her against his chest.

This was nice. He was tanned and smelled gorgeous. It would have been nicer if she hadn't been bright red in the face and wearing her painting clothes, but Clemmie could ignore that for the moment. She was safe in Gil's arms, and that was all that mattered.

'Are you okay?' His voice was laced with tenderness and concern.

'Yeah.' Her voice sounded a little weird as well, and Clemmie coughed to clear the rest of the blockage. 'What about my door?'

'The latch is broken, but it's still on its hinges. Shouldn't take too long for me to repair. Keep coughing...'

So he was staying long enough to repair the door. Right now, Clemmie couldn't care less what had brought Gil here. She just wanted him close. She coughed again, and then managed to take a deep breath without wheezing.

'That's better.' She tried to get to her feet but Gil was holding her tight. 'I'm okay now.'

He helped her up, supporting her through to the sitting room. Gil sat down on the sofa next to her, and when she leaned against his chest, he put his arm around her shoulders. That wasn't strictly necessary, but it felt good.

'What made you choke like that?'

'I…um… Do you remember when you dropped that pitcher of water and cut your hand?'

'Ah. Sorry to catch you unawares. Maybe I should have texted, rather than phoned.' Gil winced.

'No, I don't think that would have made any difference.' Clemmie was feeling better now, and she really should sit up straight. 'What are you doing here? I thought you were in Australia.'

'How did you know that?'

'I called Sam, about returning a book she'd lent me. She mentioned it.'

'I was there because… I promised you I'd go, Clemmie.'

'I shouldn't have made you promise. Since you're back so soon, it can't have been the right thing to do.' Clemmie grimaced at the thought of all that money wasted on plane tickets.

'It was the absolute right thing to do. It just didn't take as long as I thought it might. I had to talk to the people who've known me all my life to help me remember who I am. And what I can and can't do.'

He'd come to tell her that? Disappointment bloomed in Clemmie's chest and she pulled away from him. Suddenly the painting clothes *did* matter, because if she was only going to see him once more, she'd have preferred to look a little more presentable.

Then she saw the look in his eyes. Whatever he'd come for, it meant as much to Gil as it did to her.

'We should talk about this later. When you're feeling better.'

'I'm fine.' Clemmie sucked in a breath and puffed it back out again. 'See?'

'You're sure?'

This was killing her. Suddenly all she wanted was for him to say what he'd come to say and then go. He didn't even need to mend the door—that would be piling more pain onto a heart that was already hurt enough.

'I'm sure, Gil. Please will you just say whatever you're here to say.'

He nodded. 'I came back to ask you for another chance. I'm still the same man who hurt you. I always will be. I want to be the best at what I do, and I'll do whatever it takes to succeed. But my goals are different now, and I love you with all my heart. I won't leave you and I'll do whatever it takes to make you want to stay with me.'

Clemmie caught her breath. 'And once you've set your sights on something, you don't give up, do you?'

'No, I don't. You need to know that.'

It was *all* she needed to know.

'Yes, Gil.' She flung her arms around his neck, kissing him. 'We'll leave the past behind us—'

He laid his finger across her lips, smiling. 'The past is where all your strength comes from. All my determination. We're a little bit wiser than we were, though, and we know how to use what we have to make it work this time.'

'You saved my life today, Gil.'

He raised her fingers to his lips. 'I'm not sure about that. Your front door is pretty solid, and by the time I got to you, you seemed to be managing...'

Clemmie shook her head. 'I *was* managing. And you still saved my life.'

Three months later

Gil had taken Clemmie to meet his family. After just a week, they'd felt like the involved and interested family that she'd never had, and she was already looking forward to his parents' visit to London.

They'd seen the ocean and the beach. The rainforest. And then there was the grand tour that Gil had promised. They'd driven through miles of red-brown countryside, seen kangaroos, and flown across the baked heart of Australia to Sydney and then Melbourne. When Clemmie had said she wanted to see penguins, he'd taken her to Phillip Island, and when she'd wanted seafood, they'd gone to an unassuming-looking beach restaurant that served the best seafood she'd ever tasted.

But they weren't the best sights. Watching him while he slept, or opening her eyes to find that he'd been watching her, was ever fascinating. His body, wet from the shower, or hard and smooth against hers, was an endless pleasure. Gazing into his eyes, and feeling the warmth spread through her.

'Two days to go.'

Clemmie flung herself down onto the bed in their hotel room. They'd been to one of the vineyards on the Mornington Peninsula this afternoon. In the south of Australia, the early summer weather was cooler than Brisbane, and the breeze smelled of the damp earth and the vines.

'Is there anything else you want to do?' Gil grinned at her. 'There's still plenty to see.'

'Maybe we take it easy for the next couple of days.' She propped herself up on her elbows. 'We've lots to do when we get back.'

Gil nodded. 'My new research project at the rehab centre. And of course there's the cooking...'

Clemmie chuckled. They'd decided that they wanted to live in Richmond, not just because Gil's place was bigger than hers, but because they both liked the area. It meant a slightly longer commute for Clemmie, but the fast train took her into the centre of London in under half an hour. And Gil had promised to have a meal on the table every evening when she arrived home.

'You don't have to cook every night.'

'Now that your promotion's official, you'll be busy at work for a while.' Gil pulled a face. 'Don't you like my cooking?'

'I love your cooking. I just don't want you to feel you have to be home every evening to make dinner. It can tie you down a bit after a while.'

He laughed, flopping down on the bed next to her. 'You can tie me down all you want. In fact, I might insist on it.'

'Right now?' She kissed him, rolling him over onto his back and pinning his arms above his head.

'Tempting… There's something I have to do first, though. I won't be a minute.' He lifted her off him, walking through to the seating area that adjoined the bedroom. Gil had insisted on a suite, as a special treat for the last few days of their holiday.

Could she be any happier? Clemmie very much doubted it. Commitment had allowed them to talk about all the things that had torn them apart, knowing they couldn't do so again. They'd taken their time and told each other everything. It had brought Clemmie a peace that she'd never had before, and she knew that Gil was happy, too. This holiday had been one sparkling day after another, because they loved each other and they were together. It was all she needed, and all she'd ever need.

'So what's the one last thing you need to do before we leave? Perhaps we should do that tomorrow?' she asked, when Gil returned.

'I think we should do it now.' He caught her hand, pulling her to her feet and opening the sliding doors that led out onto the wide balcony.

'Oh! What a beautiful sunset!' In the short time they'd been inside, the sky had become streaked with red, outlining the dark shapes of massive gum trees. 'And champagne...'

'Clemmie.' The note of urgency in Gil's voice made her turn, and when she did she saw that he was on one knee.

'Gil!' Her hand flew to her mouth.

'Give me your hand.'

She put both of her hands into his. She was trembling now, but so was he.

'Clemmie, it's been my good fortune to meet

and fall in love with you twice. And I want to keep falling in love with you every day for the rest of my life. Will you be my wife?'

'Yes!' She pulled him to his feet, unable to wait any longer to hug him. 'When can we get married, Gil?'

He laughed, a carefree happy sound that said everything was right with his world. *Their* world.

'As soon as you like. Although I'd better give you the ring first, just to tie up all the loose ends.' He reached into his pocket, taking out a ring and slipping it onto her finger.

Clemmie caught her breath. Two diamonds flanked an opal, which sparkled with all the colours of the sunset.

'It's beautiful, Gil. Thank you.' He had that goofy, can't-help-smiling grin on his face that she loved so well, and Clemmie flung her arms around his neck, kissing him.

As the sun went down, he popped the champagne cork and handed her a glass. 'I'd like to propose a toast. To all our new adventures.'

She tipped her glass against his. 'And new adventurers.' She knew that Gil wanted children as much as she did.

He grinned. 'I'm looking forward to that, as well.'

'As soon as you like, Gil…'

His kiss told her that they wouldn't have long to wait.

* * * * *

If you missed the previous story in the Reunited at St Barnabas's Hospital duet, then check out

Twins for the Neurosurgeon
by Louisa Heaton

If you enjoyed this story, check out these other great reads from Annie Claydon

Falling for the Brooding Doc
Greek Island Fling to Forever
The Best Man and the Bridesmaid

All available now!